Also by Cal Ripken, Jr.
with Kevin Cowherd

Hothead
Super Slugger
Wild Pitch

Cal Ripken, Jr.'s
★ALL★
STARS

SQUEEZE
PLAY

a novel by
CAL RIPKEN, JR.
with Kevin Cowherd

Louisburg Library
Bringing People and Information Together

Disney • Hyperion Books
New York

First Edition
10 9 8 7 6 5 4 3 2 1
G475-5664-5-13349
Printed in the United States of America

Library of Congress Cataloging-in-Publication Data
Ripken, Cal, Jr., 1960–
Squeeze play: a novel/by Cal Ripken, Jr. and
Kevin Cowherd.—First edition.
pages cm
Summary: Centerfielder Corey Maduro has to deal with the humiliation of having an overly involved and short-tempered father in the stands.
ISBN 978-1-4231-7866-8
[1. Baseball—Fiction. 2. Fathers and sons—Fiction.] I. Cowherd, Kevin.
II. Title.
PZ7.R4842Sq 2014
[Fic]—dc23   2013019531

Reinforced binding

Visit www.disneyhyperionbooks.com

For Ed Hewitt, a great friend and baseball fan.
Thanks for all your support.
—Kevin Cowherd

Corey Maduro drifted to his left, tapped his glove with his fist, and waited for the high, lazy fly ball to descend from the sky.

"I got it!" he yelled, windmilling his arms big-league style.

This was a part of the game he loved: tracking a ball off the crack of the bat, determining its speed and trajectory, calculating the angle to take to make the catch. Not that you had to be a geometry whiz to track this one. This one was coming right at him.

Suddenly he heard footsteps. Someone was churning through the outfield grass in his direction. And closing in fast.

This can't be good, he thought, reaching up for the ball, now a foot over his head.

At that moment, a figure darted in front of him. He saw the flash of another glove, then heard the sound of the ball landing in it with a soft *whump!*

Annoyed, he looked down. It was Katelyn Morris, the Orioles right fielder.

Gee, Corey thought, what a surprise.

Katelyn whipped the ball out of her glove in a smooth motion, took a crow hop, and fired it into Justin Pryor, the second baseman. She blew on the tip of her right index finger, like it was a smoking gun, and pretended to jam it into an imaginary holster.

After shaking the long, blond hair under her cap, she turned to Corey and smiled sweetly. "See that throw?" she said. "Does this kid have an arm on her or what? I mean, that was just a rocket right there. You gotta admit that."

Corey gritted his teeth. Be cool, he told himself.

"Uh, normally when a player yells 'I got it,' that's the signal for everyone else to back off," he said. "Especially if the player yelling is the center fielder. Who is, technically, the boss of the outfield."

"Oh, did you call for it?" Katelyn asked innocently. "Guess I didn't hear. You got such a late break on the ball, I thought you needed help."

"*A late break?!*" Corey could feel his face getting hot. "I didn't have to move five feet!"

"Well, you seemed sort of paralyzed," Katelyn said. "You had that dumb look on your face. Like you didn't know what to do."

Corey stared at her with his mouth open.

"Did you ever see that commercial," she continued, "where the kid knocks over the big TV when his parents aren't home? And it cracks and sparks? And he freaks out and runs in circles around the house? You looked kind of like that kid."

Corey was about to reply when a loud voice cut the air: "Guys!"

It was Coach Mike Labriogla. He stood at home plate with a bat on his shoulder and a ball in his hand, glaring at his two outfielders.

"I'm sure you two are having a fascinating conversation," he continued. "And I'm sure there's an excellent reason why two of my players failed to communicate on a simple fly ball and nearly steamrolled each other. But maybe you could wrap it up so we can get back to practice."

Katelyn looked at Corey and shook her head. "Nice work, nerd," she hissed under her breath. "Now you got Coach mad."

"*I* got Coach mad?" Corey said. "I'm not the one who—"

But Katelyn wasn't listening. She turned and trotted back to right field.

As Coach began hitting ground balls to the infield, Corey tried to regain his concentration. But it wasn't easy. This latest brush with Hurricane Katelyn had left him as dazed and confused as all the other times.

For weeks now, she had seemed on a mission to make him look bad. Corey was a solid fielder, but on the rare occasions when he misplayed a ball in a game, Katelyn would throw her hands in the air and shoot him dirty looks from right field.

When he didn't get a hit—unfortunately, that was happening more and more, lately—she made a big show of shaking her head and muttering, "Gotta do better than that" as he trudged back to the dugout.

Oh, Katelyn was trying to show him up, all right. The only thing he couldn't figure out was why.

It wasn't as if he'd been mean to her or anything. Unlike some of the other Orioles, who didn't like a girl playing on their team and didn't try to hide it, Corey had welcomed Katelyn from the very first practice.

He knew she was a good player, for one thing. She covered a lot of ground in the outfield—okay, maybe too much at times—and had a strong, accurate throwing arm. And she was a solid hitter. Best of all, she seemed to love the game as much as he did. All that was good enough for Corey.

If you could play the game and loved baseball, he wanted you on his team. It was that simple. But Katelyn didn't seem quite as thrilled to have Corey as a teammate.

In the beginning, Corey was sure Coach would see what Katelyn was up to and tell her to knock it off. He waited for Coach to remind her that the Orioles were a team and teammates support each other; they don't criticize each other when someone makes a mistake. But Coach never had that little talk with Katelyn.

Now Corey was beginning to think that, somehow, Coach was clueless about what Katelyn was doing. Coach didn't seem oblivious about anything else. But there wasn't any other explanation at this point.

When it was time to hit, Corey jogged in to the dugout, pulled his bat from his equipment bag, and took a few warm-up swings. His best friend, shortstop Sammy Noah, sidled up to him.

"I see your good buddy Katelyn is up to her old tricks,"

he said. "That was ridiculous, dude. You had that ball all the way."

Corey smiled weakly. "Oh, she loves me," he said. "You can tell."

"Is that what it is?" Sammy said. "She has a funny way of showing it."

"Look on the bright side," Corey said. "At least she didn't spit sunflower seeds on my spikes this time."

"Or knock the ball out of your glove, like that other time," Sammy said.

"Or trip me on the bases, like she almost did when we played the Yankees," Corey said.

"Or make faces, like when you popped up that bunt against the Red Sox," Sammy said.

"See?" Corey said. "She's into me!"

"How could I have missed it?" Sammy said.

The two laughed and bumped fists. They had been best buds for years and shared the same off-kilter sense of humor. Sammy was one of the Orioles who had welcomed Katelyn initially, too. But after he'd seen how she was treating Corey, his dislike for her started growing daily.

Corey stepped into the batter's box and went through his usual routine. He dug in with his back foot, tapped the far corner of the plate to make sure he could reach an outside pitch, and settled in with his left foot. He made sure his weight was evenly balanced. But he still felt uncomfortable at the plate, as he had for a couple of weeks now.

Just then Coach stepped off the pitching rubber and announced, "Soon as batting practice is over, let's talk about the big tournament coming up."

The tournament.

Ugh. Corey felt his stomach tighten again.

The big Grand Slam Tournament was all the Orioles had talked about for weeks. They'd be traveling to a gleaming new youth-baseball complex in the town of Sea Isle, North Carolina. A colorful brochure had been sent home with each player, and the Orioles had been busily checking out the Grand Slam Web site since the beginning of the season.

What a place it was: there were no fewer than seven spectacular-looking fields, each set in a replica of a famous big-league ballpark, such as Camden Yards in Baltimore, Fenway Park in Boston, Wrigley Field in Chicago, and Yankee Stadium in New York.

There were lights for night games, tons of batting cages and practice fields—everything a baseball-loving kid could wish for.

They'd be staying in a big hotel just a long fly ball from the Atlantic Ocean, with an amusement park and Gusher World, the biggest water park in the country, almost right next door.

No wonder the Orioles were so excited. Corey had tried to pretend he was excited, too. But the truth was, he'd been dreading this trip for a while now.

Reason number one: He was in a hitting slump, maybe the worst of his Babe Ruth League career. And the thought of stringing together another dismal week of 0-for-4s at the plate wasn't exactly appealing—even in the picture-postcard setting of Sea Isle.

Reason number two: Having to put up with Katelyn

right now was hard enough. Having to put up with her on the road 24/7 would be a nightmare.

And reason number three was—

"LET'S GO, ORIOLES!" a voice boomed, interrupting his reverie. "C'MON, COREY! GET THIS TEAM GOING! SHOW SOME LIFE! YOU GUYS LOOK LIKE A BUNCH OF DEAD-HEADS OUT THERE!"

The Orioles glanced at the bleachers, where a big man with thick glasses clambered up to the top step.

Corey sighed and looked down.

Reason number three had just arrived.

Corey braced for the usual adventure on the ride home. It began almost immediately. Joe Maduro peered uncertainly out the windshield at the gathering dusk and shifted the big SUV into drive. He stomped on the gas and they lurched out of the parking lot, cutting off a minivan.

The other driver slammed on the brakes and honked the horn.

"Headlights!" Corey yelled.

"Right," his dad said, clicking them on. "Sorry."

Part of the problem, Corey realized, was that his dad's vision had gone downhill in recent years. But the other problem was that he was simply a bad driver. A really, really bad driver. The world's worst, according to Uncle Bobby, Joe Maduro's brother.

"Blind and totally clueless behind the wheel!" Uncle Bobby would cackle at family gatherings as Corey's dad shrugged sheepishly. "What a combination! And they actually let him have a license!"

Corey tugged his seat belt tighter. He would have felt

better in a full body harness, fire-retardant suit, and crash helmet, just like the NASCAR drivers had.

Except how would that look, a twelve-year-old getting into all that gear just to ride home from practice with his dad?

"You guys looked absolutely lifeless out there," Joe Maduro began as they bounced out to the main highway.

Corey looked out the window and sighed. "Dad," he said, "it's only practice."

Immediately he wished he could take it back.

"*Only* practice?" his dad said.

Corey closed his eyes. Here it comes, he thought. He'll start with Allen Iverson. . . .

"*Only* practice," his dad repeated. "Who are you, Allen Iverson?"

This, Corey knew, was a reference to the former NBA superstar who had famously delivered a rant ridiculing the importance of practice when he played for the Philadelphia 76ers years ago.

Corey's dad had found it on YouTube and made him watch it again and again. Each time, Joe Maduro had snorted with disgust when it was over and said, "Can you believe that guy? What, he's so good he doesn't have to work at it?"

"What do I always tell you about practice?" Corey's dad continued now. "Huh? What do I always say?"

"Here come the Six *P*'s," Corey whispered to himself. The traffic was heavy now. His eyes widened with alarm as the SUV drifted to the shoulder of the road.

"The Six *P*'s, right?" his dad said. "Proper Practice Prevents Piss-Poor Performance. How many times have we gone over that?"

Only about a hundred, Corey thought. Not that anyone's counting.

Suddenly a shower of gravel sprayed the side of their car. Corey's dad swore softly. He tugged the steering wheel hard to the left and they careened back onto the highway.

"Uh, Dad?" Corey said, heart beating faster now. "Can we keep it on the road?"

"Why don't you let me drive, big guy," his dad said. "You worry about your team, okay? The way you Orioles look, it's like you don't even care!"

Why should I worry about the team? Corey thought. You worry about it enough for both of us.

He looked out the window again and watched as the familiar landscape whizzed by: the Welkin Farms tree nursery, the Ed Ross Chevrolet dealership, Rosie's Diner, with its huge neon sign proclaiming HOME OF THE WORLD'S BEST FRIES!

Corey loved his dad, loved him with all his heart. But lately it seemed as if all Joe Maduro wanted to talk about was the Orioles. He was supercritical of everything Corey did on the baseball field, too, harping on every little mistake. Now his dad was even showing up to watch the team practice.

None of the other dads seemed so wrapped up in the Orioles, not even Mr. Noah, who was proud of the fact that he'd never missed one of Sammy's games, dating back to T-ball.

Corey's dad had always been his biggest fan, and Corey appreciated that. But these days Joe Maduro was always questioning the umpires whenever a call went against the Orioles. Not only that, he also heckled the other teams and got into arguments with the other players' parents.

It was embarrassing. And it was getting worse and worse. Everyone on the Orioles was beginning to notice.

"The team's going to be fine, Dad," Corey said finally. "Coach said we looked sharp during infield and outfield. And everyone was killing it in batting practice."

"Good," his dad said, smiling for the first time since he'd arrived at practice.

Corey left out the details about Katelyn robbing him of a fly ball and Coach barking at the two of them, figuring this would only get his dad riled up again and lead to another rant about practice habits. Which wouldn't be good, seeing as how they were already drifting into another lane.

It was Sammy who had first dubbed these drives "Death Rides." When Corey's mom was alive, she would sit up front with his dad, and Corey and Sammy would sit in the back and giggle whenever his mother gasped, grabbed the dashboard, and cried, "Joe! Slow down! It's a red light!"

But that was years ago. Now that his mom was gone and he was big enough to sit up front, watching his dad weave all over the road wasn't funny anymore.

At times—like now—it could be downright terrifying.

"Are you fired up about the tournament?" his dad asked. "You guys are playing some pretty good teams. That team from Virginia? The Norfolk Red Sox? They're supposed to have great pitching."

Corey groaned inwardly. No! Could it be? Was his dad actually scouting the other teams in the tournament?

This, Corey thought, was the whole problem with the Internet. Anyone could get information about anything at any time. For an instant, he fantasized about taking his dad's laptop when he wasn't home and tossing it in the nearest Dumpster. Or climbing onto the roof of their house and sailing it Frisbee-style until it crashed on the sidewalk below.

"I figure it's about a six-hour ride to Sea Isle," his dad said, draping a beefy hand over the steering wheel. "Coach talked about carpooling. Tell him I volunteer to drive. See if Sammy and his dad want to come with us. It'll be fun. We'll all have plenty of time to talk about the team."

Corey looked out the window again. He tried to imagine six hours trapped in a car while his dad droned on and on about the tournament, and about the Orioles and how crappy they practiced, and how they were going to get their butts beaten so badly. No, there weren't enough pit stops for burgers and ice cream cones to make that bearable.

A flash of light caused him to swing his eyes back to the road. A big eighteen-wheeler was emerging from the service road on their right. But his dad wasn't slowing down. Corey gasped and grabbed the dashboard.

"Dad!" he shouted. "That truck is—"

His dad stomped on the brakes and veered into the far left lane. Somewhere behind them, tires squealed.

Corey closed his eyes. Why am I stressing about the tournament? he thought. We'll probably never make it there alive.

The Orioles' going-away party was held at Coach's
rambling farmhouse, which sat next to a small pond that
shimmered in the afternoon sunlight. A large banner hung
from the porch railing. Painted in orange and black letters,
it said: GOOD LUCK, ORIOLES! HAVE A GREAT TOURNAMENT!

Mr. Noah dropped off Sammy and Corey at two o'clock.
Mickey Labriogla, Coach's son, greeted them at the door,
chomping on the biggest hamburger either of them had
ever seen.

"How do you even get that thing in your mouth?" Corey
asked.

"It looks like a cannonball between two buns," Sammy
said.

"Made it myself," Mickey said, grinning. "Mushed three
burgers into one. Dad fired it up on the grill."

"The kid's a genius!" Sammy said. "Wish I had thought
of that."

Mickey was the Orioles catcher, a thickly built boy
with a smile that seemed permanently on display. But as

good-natured as Mickey was, the Orioles knew he was all business on a baseball diamond.

No one in the league was better at blocking pitches in the dirt and leaping for errant fastballs over the batter's head. No catcher had a better arm and none blocked the plate as ferociously as Mickey did, either. Corey had seen countless base runners slide into Mickey's shin guards trying to score, only to be stopped dead in their tracks. It was like sliding into a brick chimney with legs.

"Here's today's program, sports fans," Mickey said, ushering them inside and wiping ketchup from his mouth with his sleeve. "Burgers and hot dogs are cooking out back. A couple of the guys are shooting baskets. And we'll get a Wiffle ball game going as soon as everyone gets here.

"If I were you," he continued, patting his ample belly, "I'd go for the food first. But that's just me."

"You? Go for the food?" Sammy said, nudging Corey. "That's hard to believe."

Mickey glared at him in mock outrage.

"Now look what you did, Sammy!" Corey said. "You hurt his feelings!"

"Hey, it's not like I've been piggin' out!" Mickey said. "Ask my dad. This is only my first burger!"

"Or third," Sammy said. "Depending on how you do the math."

"I'm counting it as one," Mickey said, the grin returning. "My house, my rules."

They followed Mickey out into the backyard, where Coach presided over a hot grill, plumes of smoke circling his head. He wore an orange Orioles T-shirt, black sweat-pants, and a big, floppy chef's hat. He waved to them with a big spatula in one hand.

"Don't ask me to make what he's eating," Coach growled, pointing the spatula at Mickey, who popped the last of his burger in his mouth. "The boy could wipe out the entire ground-beef aisle at Sam's Club."

"A small price to pay for the privilege of coaching the best catcher in the league!" Mickey said. He flexed his biceps and danced about wildly, which cracked up every-one, even Coach.

Soon the rest of the team arrived and the yard was a sea of noise as the Orioles talked excitedly about the upcoming tournament and their week in North Carolina.

After lunch, most of them played two-on-two basket-ball, switching teams every six points so everyone got in. Corey was having such a good time he almost forgot he was the only Oriole *not* looking forward to the tournament.

But when they stopped playing and plopped down in the cool grass to rest, a strange feeling came over him.

There was something different about this cookout, he thought, something that made it even more fun than the others they'd had. Something he couldn't quite put his fin-ger on . . .

Then it hit him: Katelyn wasn't there.

Yes, that was it. No one had called him nerd, or pointed out his lack of table manners, or complained about how much ketchup he'd slathered on his burger. And when they had played hoops, no one had elbowed him in the ribs as he went up for a rebound, or hooted when he missed a jump shot.

He glanced around the Labrioglas' backyard again, thinking he might have missed Katelyn with all the Orioles running around. But no, there was no sign of her.

"Where's Wonder Girl?" he asked Sammy.

"She's not here?" Sammy said, scanning the crowd. "Hmm, you're right. Now, why is that?" He scrambled to his feet. "As the great Harry Potter said, 'We must investigate! Follow me, Ron Weasley!'"

They found Coach still hard at work over the grill. Beads of perspiration dotted his red face as he fired up the last half-dozen burgers for anyone still hungry.

"Coach," Sammy said casually, "where's our star right fielder?"

"Couldn't make it," Coach said, fanning smoke from his eyes. "Apparently she's not feeling well."

Corey and Sammy looked at each other, then quickly lowered their eyes, trying not to smile.

"Gee, that's too bad," Sammy said at last.

Coach nodded gravely. "Her mom says Katelyn's pretty sick," he added. "Could be the flu. She might miss the whole tournament, poor kid."

"Oh," Corey said, hoping he sounded sincere. "That would be . . . *terrible.*"

Actually, he thought, it *would* be terrible. Katelyn was definitely one of the Orioles' best players, and one of their fastest base runners, too. Only Hunter Carlson, the skinny third baseman, had more steals, a fact that seemed to annoy Katelyn no end. Maybe that was why she seemed to resent Hunter almost as much as she resented Corey.

Still, the thought of her staying home with a runny nose, hacking cough, and 102-degree fever did not exactly bring tears to Corey's eyes.

Coach shrugged. "Playing without her would be tough," he said. "But we'd just have to do the best we can. There's still a lot of talent on this team, boys. You know how NFL teams like the Ravens are always talking about 'next man up'? How when a player goes down with an injury, someone else has to step up and carry the load? That's how it has to be with the Orioles this week if Katelyn can't make it."

Corey and Sammy nodded, trying to keep a straight face. But as soon as they were out of Coach's sight, they grinned at each other and bumped fists. From a personal point of view, Corey thought "next man up" without Katelyn was sounding pretty good.

The Wiffle ball game was the highlight of the afternoon. They chose teams and played in a big field near the pond. Corey, Sammy, Hunter, and Gabe Vasquez, the Orioles' best pitcher, called themselves the Supreme Sluggers. Mickey, Justin, left fielder Spencer Dalton, first baseman Ethan Novitsky, and outfielder/pitcher Danny Connolly, the smallest kid on the Orioles, were the O's Elites.

With the score tied at 9–9, two outs, and the bases loaded in the sixth inning, Hunter crossed up the Elites by laying down a beautiful bunt that died in the grass in front of the pitcher's mound.

As Mickey stumbled after the ball and threw too late

to first base, Sammy crossed home plate with the winning run, his hands raised in triumph. As the Sluggers whooped and traded high fives, the Elites howled in protest.

"Who bunts in Wiffle ball?" Hunter demanded. "Are you even allowed to do that?"

"Smart, aggressive teams bunt," Sammy said. "Teams that aren't afraid to push the envelope."

Spencer snorted. "Only wusses bunt in Wiffle ball."

"Yeah," Danny said. "And you have the nerve to call yourselves the Supreme *Sluggers*?"

"The Sluggers are not bound by a single way to win, my tiny friend," Gabe said. "If we have to crush the ball, we crush the ball. But if we have to drop a bunt on your sleepy butts, we'll do that, too."

"Wait, did you just call Danny your tiny friend?" Spencer asked with a grin.

"Well, I don't know whether you've noticed," Gabe said, "but he's not exactly Shaquille O'Neal. He's about the size of one of Shaq's sneakers."

By now, players on both teams were laughing. It reminded Corey of the backyard games of tennis-ball Home Run Derby he'd played with the neighborhood kids when he was younger. Arguing about the ground rules and trash-talking with the other team was as much fun as actually playing.

A moment later, Coach broke up the discussion by calling them together.

"Boys, we leave for Sea Isle promptly at nine a.m. tomorrow," he said. "You all know who you're carpooling with. The tournament begins the next day. We're playing five games in seven days against some top-flight teams, so it'll give us a chance to see just how good we are.

"We want to play our best baseball down there," Coach continued. "In fact, we want to win the championship. I think we're that good. But win or lose, the main thing is to have fun. We want to come away from this tournament with lots of great memories."

At that moment, Corey wished he had a recording device so he could play Coach's words back for his dad. You mean baseball could be fun? Win or lose? Corey was pretty sure Joe Maduro did not exactly share that philosophy.

No, most of the time baseball seemed more like war than a game to his dad. And Corey couldn't imagine that would change just because they were playing in a spectacular venue.

But a few minutes later, as he climbed into Mr. Noah's car for the ride home, Corey tried to think positively, the way his mom had taught him.

If his bat came around even a little, if Katelyn wasn't around to annoy him, if his dad would only calm down and not act like such a wild man during games, maybe the tournament wouldn't be so bad.

But Corey knew those were three big ifs. And right now he was feeling squeezed by all three.

He sighed and stared out the window at the white, puffy clouds gliding across the bright blue sky. Mom, he thought, I'm trying. I really am.

Corey wondered if he had died and gone to baseball heaven.

He stared at the perfectly manicured field that stretched out before him. The grass was as green and clipped as the felt on a pool table. The red clay of the base paths looked so smooth it was as if every last pebble and errant clump of dirt had been permanently banished.

Forget having a ground ball go through your legs and telling your coach, "The ball took a bad hop." That wouldn't work here. For some reason, this thought made Corey sad. Bad hops were the age-old excuse of every shaky fielder he had ever known.

Now you couldn't use that one anymore? What was the world coming to?

"Welcome to Camden Yards—well, our version of it, anyway." Their Grand Slam tour guide, a gangly teenager named Josh, spoke in a bored voice. "What you're looking at is Prescription Athletic Turf, the same used in the iconic stadium in Baltimore. Like that one, our field has a state-of-the-art irrigation and sprinkler system. Same goes for the drainage system. Layer upon layer of intersecting pipes means it could pretty much rain all day and fifteen minutes after it stopped, this field would be good to go."

"Sweet!" Sammy said.

But he wasn't listening to Josh drone on about irrigation and drainage pipes. Instead, Sammy gazed at the replica of the famous ballpark's warehouse beyond the right field wall, seemingly close enough to touch.

"Tell you what, I plan to launch a few balls off that baby," he said. "Don't *you* even think about it, Maduro. That's only for us big boys."

Corey smiled as a warm ocean breeze wafted over them.

"Who am I, one of the Smurfs?" Corey said. "And you're, like, Miguel Cabrera all of a sudden? Well, go for it, dude. Just don't let Coach hear you. You know what he thinks about guys trying to jack homers. And how it messes up their swings."

Corey was in a good mood. The long ride to North Carolina had proven to be surprisingly uneventful, even if it had taken Mr. Noah about ten seconds to sense that Joe Maduro was not the greatest driver in the world and that this could be the last ride any of them would ever take.

But while Corey and Sammy had spent the trip talking, watching movies, and playing video games in the backseat, Mr. Noah had somehow managed to carry on a running conversation with Corey's dad about everything from sports to politics to the economy while also quietly pointing out potential traffic hazards when the other man's concentration seemed to wane.

"Uh, getting a little close on the right here, Joe," Sammy's dad had said at one point, and Corey marveled at how calm the man sounded as they drifted toward a Greyhound bus in the other lane.

"Might want to move over and let this rig merge," Mr. Noah had said another time as Corey's dad roared up on an eighteen-wheeler entering the highway from a rest stop.

Even when Joe Maduro went on a rant about the tournament and how the Orioles had no chance of doing well if they didn't start focusing and taking practice more seriously, Mr. Noah was able to steer the talk back to something lighter, something that didn't make Corey's dad grip the steering wheel so hard his knuckles turned white.

Wish I could calm him down like that, Corey thought. It would make the rides home from games way more pleasant. But he sensed that this was a kind of skill you didn't master until you were much older, maybe after high school.

Once on the island they had checked into their hotel, the Sand Dune, a towering, bone-white structure just one block from the ocean. Both boys had been delighted to see the huge swimming pool out back, with a "lazy river" for tubing and raft-riding, as well as a full game room with Ping-Pong, pool tables, and video games.

Now Corey, Sammy, and some of the other Orioles— Corey was relieved to see a certain blond-haired right fielder not among them—were getting their first look at the eye-popping Grand Slam facilities. They toured the other six replica fields, stopping to read the informational plaque on the history of each distinctive major-league stadium and some of the big games that were played there.

As they passed a series of bull-pen mounds and bunting stations, Josh suddenly stopped.

For the first time since the tour began, he seemed excited. "See that big pond over there?" he said, pointing at a muddy circle of water surrounded by marsh grass and scrub pine off in the distance. "You do not—I repeat *not*— want to go near that."

The Orioles looked quizzically at one another, then back at Josh.

"Okay," Mickey said finally. "Why?"

Josh lowered his voice dramatically. "Because there's an alligator in there. A big twelve-foot gator named Freddy. And he's mean and ornery and scary-looking. Not to mention hungry most of the time."

"A real, live alligator?" Justin said with alarm. "What does he eat?"

Josh smiled mysteriously but didn't answer. Finally he said, "Okay, tour's over, guys." He nodded in the direction of the big pavilion where they had entered. "You can meet up with your coach and parents over there."

After Josh left, the Orioles retraced their steps, animatedly discussing the level of threat Freddy the Gator posed. It was quickly decided that if Freddy were to eat any of them, it would most likely be Danny, since his short, stubby legs made him the slowest kid on the team.

"*Me?*" Danny said in a quavering voice. "Why does he have to eat *me*? Why can't he eat Justin? Justin's only a little bigger than I am."

"I'm *way* bigger than you are, shrimp," Justin said hotly.

"He'd probably eat both of you," Gabe said. "Look, you're

both about the size of small dogs, right? And you always hear about alligators picking off small dogs that wander too close to a pond or a swamp or whatever."

"All I know," Justin said, pointing to Danny, "is I can outrun *him*. And that's all I'd have to do if Freddy comes after us."

By now they were all laughing and hooting and enjoying the warm sunshine as they cut through the Camden Yards replica outfield again.

Suddenly something slammed against the overhead scoreboard with a loud *BAM!* Instinctively, they all ducked, only to see a baseball drop harmlessly at their feet. A high-pitched cackle sounded from somewhere behind them.

They whirled around. Corey groaned.

There, running up to them and grinning wildly, was Katelyn. A huge wad of bubble gum bulged in one cheek as she bent down with her glove to retrieve the ball.

"Welcome to Sea Isle, nerds!" she sang out. "I thought you'd never get here!"

Sammy stared at her, slack-jawed. Finally he said: "Weren't you, like, dying of the flu?"

Katelyn shrugged and blew a big pink bubble that popped loudly. She squeezed in between Corey and Sammy and draped an arm around each boy.

"Hey, I'm not feeling the love!" she said. "If I didn't know better, I'd almost think you're not happy to see me!"

The ball came whistling out of the pitching machine belt-high, just the way Corey liked it. He turned on it—hips, shoulders, arms rotating—and tried to take a level cut. But he was late getting the bat around, and the result was a weak shot into the right side of the net.

"Okay, that wasn't . . . *horrible*," Sammy said.

Corey grunted and lowered his bat. "Tell me the truth," he said. "Was it a base hit?"

Sammy cocked his head and appeared to study the angle at which the ball had caught the netting. "All right, here's my feeling," he said. "If the kid playing second base was really, really short? Like if he was seven years old? Then it was a base hit."

He exploded with laughter and collapsed on a nearby bench.

Corey sighed and got ready for the next pitch. "That's great," he said. "The way I'm hitting, I *will* be playing with seven-year-olds soon."

"Hey, then you can play with Benny!" Sammy said, referring to his younger brother. "They'll probably even let you bat cleanup. Dude, I bet you even make the all star team!"

Corey glared at him, but Sammy was laughing so hard again he didn't notice.

The Orioles were getting in some batting practice in preparation for the Skills Competition that night and their first game the next morning. The players had taken over the twenty pitching machines and batting cages, all in pristine condition, that were spread across the back of the Grand Slam complex.

Coach had suggested the extra BP as a way to work off nervous energy on their first day in North Carolina, and the Orioles had jumped at the opportunity. But now Corey was getting increasingly frustrated with his inability to put a good swing on the ball. He wasn't hitting any better here than he had been back home. And with five games over the next week, the prospect of going 0-for-Sea-Isle in a big tournament was making him anxious.

He fouled off two more pitches, then hit a soft dribbler up the middle that clanked off the leg of the pitching machine. On the next two pitches he swung so hard that he missed them completely, his head flying off the ball on both.

"Somebody *please* tell me what I'm doing wrong!" he muttered, throwing the bat down in frustration.

"Oh, that's easy, Maduro," a voice behind him said. "You're trying to be a hitter. And we all know how that's been working out."

Corey turned to find Katelyn leaning against her bat behind the cage, grinning.

"Look who's here," Sammy said, leaping off the bench. "I didn't know they were shooting *Mean Girls 3* today."

"Very funny, nerd," Katelyn said. "Who helped you think of that one? No way you came up with it by yourself."

She picked up her bat and took a couple of vicious swings, the bat making whistling sounds as it cut through the air.

"Let me know if you need a lesson in there, Maduro," she said. "From the looks of things, you definitely do."

Corey fumed. Katelyn had been making nasty little digs at him for weeks, and for all that time he'd been working hard to control his temper around her. But now he was sick and tired of all the shots.

"Okay, I'm in a little slump," he said hotly. "But you couldn't hit with me on your best day."

Katelyn's grin vanished. Her eyes narrowed. "Oh?" she said, tapping the head of the bat against her hand. "Then how 'bout we have a little hitting contest? Unless you're too scared."

"Bring it," Corey said. "Anytime. Anywhere."

By now, a few more Orioles had gathered around the cage, drawn by the sound of raised voices. Corey could feel his hands starting to sweat. This wouldn't be easy, not the way he was swinging the bat.

Katelyn was one of the best hitters on the team, too. Corey had more power—he was the Orioles number five hitter, after all, and she batted second. But he was feeling so lost at the plate these days that even Benny Noah or one of his little buddies could probably strike him out.

Still, there was no backing down now. Not with everyone standing around looking at them and nudging one another as if a schoolyard fight was about to break out.

"Okay, Maduro," Katelyn said. "How 'bout we do it right now? Here's how it's going to work. We each hit ten balls. Whoever has the most hits wins. Loser buys the winner ice cream back at the hotel. Which means you'll be buying me a mint chocolate chip cone."

She stepped back and took another savage swing.

"With three scoops."

She took another swing.

"And sprinkles."

"Ooooooh," the rest of the Orioles murmured. *"Sprinkles!"*

"You're on," Corey said, laughing at his teammates despite his nerves. "But how do we tell who has the most hits? After all, we're hitting into a net. . . ."

"Easy," Katelyn said. "We get somebody to be the judge."

"How about Sammy?" Corey said. "He's the most honest kid I know. He's like the Mount Everest of integrity. He's kind, brave, loyal—"

"Not to mention handsome in a James Franco sort of way," Sammy interrupted, taking off his cap and smoothing his hair.

Katelyn snorted. "Nice try, Maduro. Like I'm gonna let you pick your best bud. No way."

Corey threw his hands up and said, "Fine. Pick one of the other guys."

Katelyn gazed at the rest of the Orioles and wrinkled her nose. "These goofs? Puh-leeze! No, we need someone who's totally impartial. And I know just the person. Be right back."

She disappeared around the corner and returned a moment later with Coach in tow.

"Let the games begin!" he bellowed, rubbing his hands together. "A batting contest? This is my kind of competition! Who's up first?"

Katelyn elbowed Corey aside and said, "Beauty before—well, whatever it is you have, Maduro."

She sauntered into the cage and made a big deal of putting on her batting gloves, pulling down on each finger until it was just so, and tightening and untightening the Velcro fasteners at each wrist.

Next she reached into her back pocket and pulled out a packet of Big League Chew, slowly tapping the shredded pink bubble gum into her mouth until it became a wad the size of a golf ball.

Then she picked up her bat and took a couple of swings to get loose.

"Any time now, Katelyn," Coach said, winking at the rest of the Orioles. "Think they turn the lights out at midnight."

As everyone chuckled, Katelyn shot Coach a glare and stepped in. She dropped into an athletic stance, bending slightly at the knees and holding the bat high, waving it in tiny circles as she waited.

"Ten swings," Coach said, pulling a pen and notepad from his pocket. "I'll do my best to determine if it would've been a base hit. Here we go."

The balls shot out in ten-second intervals. Katelyn put on a show. She made good contact on almost every pitch and sprayed shots to every part of the net. When she was through, she walked up to Corey, jabbed him in the chest with her forefinger, and said, "I changed my mind. Make it vanilla fudge ripple."

"Ooooh, vanilla fudge ripple!" the Orioles repeated.

Corey stepped in and was surprised by how calm he felt. Maybe it was because his teammates were relaxed, kidding around with Katelyn. Whatever it was, instead of holding the bat with the death grip he'd used for weeks, he held it loosely. He concentrated on seeing the ball the whole way and keeping his head still.

Quick, compact swing, he told himself. Just hit it hard. And now he seemed to be on every pitch, meeting the ball on the sweet spot of the bat, pulling it and driving it up the middle consistently.

From behind him, he heard murmurs of approval. He was hitting better than he had in a long time, and everyone could see it. It was as if a light switch had been turned on and the mechanics of hitting were no longer shrouded in mystery.

After the last pitch, the rest of the Orioles cheered and broke into chants of: "COR-EE! COR-EE!"

Coach scribbled a few more notations and held up his hands for quiet.

"Okay, here's the final tally," he said. "Katelyn did an absolutely terrific job. I gave her"—here he paused for dramatic effect—"five sure hits."

"Only *five*?" Katelyn cried. This set off a chorus of boos, to which she responded by sticking out her tongue.

"As for Corey," Coach continued, "also a terrific piece of hitting. Best I've seen from him in quite a while. Wish he'd do that in the games. And for him I have—drum roll, please—six hits!"

"YES!" the Orioles cried, pounding Corey on the back as he did a little fist pump in celebration.

"Therefore," Coach continued, "by the power vested in me, I hereby declare Corey the winner of whatever goofy side bet you guys made."

"You're so freakin' lucky, Maduro," Katelyn snarled. She threw her bat into her equipment bag and began angrily peeling off her gloves.

"I think I'll go with chocolate marshmallow," Corey said loudly.

"Ooooh, *chocolate marshmallow*!" the Orioles intoned.

Katelyn grabbed her bag and started to walk away, but Corey tapped her on the shoulder.

"Oh, and three scoops," he added.

Again she started to walk away. Again he tapped her on the shoulder. "With sprinkles," he said.

"Ooooh, *sprinkles*!" the Orioles said.

As he watched her stomp away, her gear bag swinging from her shoulder, Corey couldn't help smiling with satisfaction.

Ticking off Katelyn was probably not going to make his life any easier this week.

But at the moment it sure was fun.

Corey looked around at the packed stands, the bright lights, and the big video board that screamed HOME RUN DERBY! and felt his hands sweating.

The crowd was buzzing with excitement. The Home Run Derby was the marquee event of the Skills Competition. One player from each team was chosen to compete. And an hour earlier, at a special team meeting, Coach had an announced that the player representing the Orioles would be none other than—ta-da!—Corey Maduro.

Which had prompted Corey to wonder if Coach had actually lost his mind.

He glanced now at the other players in the competition. They were scattered all around the backstop, wearing confident smiles and joking with teammates as they stretched, took warm-up swings, or examined their bats.

"What am I doing here?" Corey said, licking his lips nervously.

"Dude, you're the best long-ball hitter on the team," Sammy said. "Why *wouldn't* you be here?"

"Oh, let me see," Corey said. "How about the fact that I'm, like, zero-for-June?"

Sammy shrugged. "A mere detail."

"Or the fact that I haven't exactly been crushing the ball like Josh Hamilton that whole time," Corey said.

"Totally not important," Sammy said.

"Totally not important? In a home-run contest? Are you serious?"

Sammy clapped him on the back. "You didn't look zero-for-June against Katelyn today. You looked like the old Corey, son! I wouldn't stress it. Coach knows what he's doing."

That was the part Corey didn't get. Coach generally *did* know what he was doing. But this move, sticking a slump-ridden kid in a Home Run Derby, didn't seem to make sense.

"We've got a lot of faith in you, Corey," Coach had said earlier. "You're getting your stroke back. I can feel it. You were crushing it in the cage earlier. Go after it the same way in the homer contest.

"Besides," he'd added with a wink, "guess who's pitching to you? Me! I'll make those pitches so fat you'll think you're back in T-ball again."

Actually, Corey *did* find that comforting. Coach was a terrific pitcher at batting practice, with great control and an uncanny knack for putting the ball exactly where each Oriole hitter liked it. Corey wondered if that didn't sometimes mess up the Orioles during games, when they faced pitchers who were wild and weren't grooving the ball, and were actually trying to get them out.

But he was definitely happy Coach was pitching to him

here, because he knew he could take the old man deep. He'd done it many times in BP.

"Did you notice your biggest fan is here?" Sammy asked. He jerked his head in the direction of the bleachers directly behind them. Corey turned and saw Katelyn sitting next to her mom four rows up. She was glaring right at him.

"Here's a shocker: she doesn't look happy to see me," Corey said.

Sammy nodded. "Yeah, she's been telling everyone she should be in this contest instead of you."

"Why don't I find that surprising?" Corey said.

Earlier, Katelyn, along with Sammy and Mickey, had been in the Relay Contest, in which the team that fired the ball the quickest from the warning track to home plate won.

But their team had finished a distant eleventh, mainly because Sammy had trouble pulling one throw out of the webbing of his glove, and the normally sure-handed Mickey had dropped another throw at the plate.

Sammy's theory was that a seething Katelyn had decided to sit as close to Corey as possible, in the hope that all of the rotten luck that had befallen the Relay team would now befall him.

"I'm waiting for her to make a slicing motion across her throat to the judges when you're up," Sammy said, which made them both crack up.

Just then, the public-address system crackled to life.

"LADIES AND GENTLEMEN, BOYS AND GIRLS, LET'S GET THIS THING GOING!" the announcer intoned.

"Okay," Sammy said. "Show them some Orioles power. You can totally do this."

The two traded fist bumps and Sammy squeezed into a front-row seat in the stands next to his dad and Corey's father. Corey was relieved to see the three of them sitting together. Mr. Noah definitely seemed to have a calming influence on Joe Maduro. Hopefully, Corey thought, Dad won't yell something horrible—at me or anyone else—that'll make me want to die right here.

The rules for the Home Run Derby were simple. Each hitter got seven "outs." An "out" was any swing that didn't result in a homer over the fence in fair territory. Whoever had the most homers would be declared the winner.

He checked the batting-order list and groaned. There it was: Corey Maduro, dead last. Great. What were the odds? But then he tried to think positively, as his mom had always taught. Going last would give him time to settle down. It might even help him pick up a tip or two from the better hitters in the contest. It might help him avoid some of the mistakes of the other hitters, too.

Right away he saw there were some big kids in the contest, many of them swinging fancy composite bats with barrels the size of tree trunks. Some of those bats cost hundreds of dollars, and Corey knew he wouldn't be getting one soon. His dad thought it was ridiculous to spend that kind of money on a bat. "If you can hit, you can hit with a bamboo pole," he always said.

As he watched kid after kid come to the plate, Corey felt his confidence growing. Most of them were making the classic mistake of trying to kill the ball. They were taking wild, looping swings at their coaches' pitches. And for the most part, the result was a succession of harmless pop-ups and balls beaten into the dirt. There would be oohs and aahs from the crowd after each swing, invariably followed by groans of disappointment when the ball didn't sail over the fence.

Only a tall, blond-haired kid from Ohio and a redheaded kid from Pennsylvania put decent swings on the ball. Each cracked three homers to tie for the lead. And the take-away Corey got from watching each kid was this: Have patience up there. Stay within yourself.

Finally, after what felt like an eternity, it was his turn.

"NOW BATTING, FROM THE DULANEY ORIOLES, COR-EE MAH-DOO-ROW!" trilled the PA guy, dragging it out like they did in the big leagues.

Corey dug in and felt the same eerie calmness come over him that he'd felt in the batting cage. He looked out at Coach, who gave him a wink. Coach slid his hand across his belly and Corey nodded.

Message understood: belt-high fastballs on the way Pitches your grandma could jack out of the park if she didn't get stupid and overswing.

Corey did neither.

CRACK! He turned on Coach's first pitch and launched it over the left field fence.

CRACK! The second pitch landed ten feet to the right of the first one.

CRACK! He hit a long soaring rainbow that cleared the center field fence by fifteen feet.

"OH, MY!" the PA guy cried. "THE BOY'S PUTTING ON A CLINIC!"

Three pitches. Three homers. The crowd was going

wild. Corey could hear Sammy's excited voice above the din. He stepped out of the batter's box and stole a quick glance at his dad. Joe Maduro was smiling and clapping along with everyone else.

Smiling and clapping is good, Corey thought. He hadn't seen much of that from his dad this season—especially when he was playing crappy.

Then, suddenly, Corey's bat went cold.

He topped the next two pitches and neither made it out of the infield. Relax, he told himself. Level swing. Wait on it. But he topped the next pitch, too, and now he felt himself pressing slightly.

When he lunged at the last pitch and hit a feeble pop-up that died in the glove of a kid behind second base, a murmur of disappointment went through the stands.

"QUITE A PERFORMANCE FROM YOUNG MR. MADURO!" the announcer said. "AND WE HAVE A THREE-WAY TIE IN THE HOME RUN DERBY! ROUND TWO COMING UP!"

"You'll get 'em now, Corey!" Sammy shouted. But when Corey looked back, his dad was frowning and shaking his head.

In round two, each player had only five "outs." But the first two batters seemed worn out now, their adrenaline spent. The tall kid from Ohio hit four ground balls and finally homered on his last swing, the ball barely making it over the fence in left field. The boy from Pennsylvania topped all five pitches for no homers and hurled his bat in disgust.

Corey took a deep breath. It was showtime. Two decent swings and he could win this thing.

As soon as he stepped to the plate, the crowd began clapping rhythmically, hoping for a repeat of his three-swing magic from the first round.

Coach was still serving up pitches exactly where Corey wanted them, pitches a second grader could airmail. But something was different about this at-bat. Corey could feel that his timing was off.

He just missed on the first two pitches, sending two drives to the warning track as the crowd groaned each time. His third swing was a solid line drive to left, which would have been great in a game, just not in a home-run contest.

Two "outs" left. He needed back-to-back homers to win.

"QUIT FOOLING AROUND, COREY!" a voice yelled. "YOU SHOULD HAVE WRAPPED THIS UP ALREADY!"

Thanks, Dad, he thought. Way to ease the pressure.

But his next swing produced a two-hopper to short. One "out" left. One homer needed to tie and force a third round. But on his last swing, he sent a towering fly ball to center field as the kid from Ohio raised his hands in triumph.

"AND ROBBIE ORMACH FROM THE YOUNGSVILLE BRAVES WINS THIS YEAR'S HOME RUN DERBY!" the announcer said. "LET'S HAVE A BIG ROUND OF APPLAUSE FOR ALL THREE FINALISTS!"

The kid from Ohio tipped his cap and waved to the crowd. Moments later, they were handing him a gleaming gold trophy that was almost as tall as he was, and he was posing for photographers with his mom and dad and his coach.

Corey stood off to one side and watched silently, trying to sort out his feelings.

On the one hand, he was definitely disappointed. That big trophy could have been his—*should* have been his. But for the first time in a long time, he was feeling encouraged by how well he was hitting the ball.

Maybe Coach was right, he told himself. Maybe he was coming out of his slump. Maybe he'd finally start driving in some runs and help the Orioles win a few games down here.

He looked at the stands and saw Sammy and Mr. Noah waving at him. But his dad was gone. Corey wasn't surprised. Dad wasn't crazy about kids who finished second or third. He was probably in the car now, waiting to tell Corey all the things he did wrong on the ride back to the hotel.

He felt a tap on his shoulder. It was Katelyn, flashing a big smile.

"I feel bad for you, Maduro," she said. "No, really. You came so close, too."

Yeah, he thought as he watched her walk away. You really look brokenhearted.

The Orioles' first game was on Wrigley Field—a replica of the Chicago park—against the Dover Cardinals, a Delaware team with jerseys emblazoned with the logo of a fierce-looking red bird.

"Looks more like a pissed-off pterodactyl than a cardinal," Spencer said as they watched the Cardinals take infield.

"Like you're a big pterodactyl expert," Ethan snapped.

Spencer shot him a look and said, "You don't have to be an expert to see that's not exactly a little seed-eating bird. That thing would eat a cow."

"Oh, so now you're an expert on birds, too," Ethan said.

"Hey, Ethan," Spencer said. "Do me a favor, okay? Disappear. Like for good."

The Orioles were tense. Corey could see it in everyone's faces as he scanned the dugout. Most of his teammates were pounding their gloves, and chewing their gum hard enough to make their teeth crack. And the ones who weren't were nervously tapping their bats against the cement floor and shoveling sunflower seeds into their mouths as if the world's supply was about to dry up any minute.

Coach apparently could sense the mood, too.

"What's the matter with you guys?" he said. "We're supposed to be having *fun*, remember? This is baseball, not homework. It's a game! You've been playing it all your lives. This game's no different than all the ones we've played back home."

The Orioles nodded weakly. Corey noticed that even rough, tough Katelyn seemed jittery. As Coach spoke, she tried to smile. But it looked as if her face might crack from the effort.

Coach read the batting order. Corey saw he was still hitting in the number five hole. It was a testament to Coach's boundless faith in him, even though his dad had grumbled after the home-run contest that Corey "couldn't hit a beach ball right now."

". . . and Gabe pitching and batting number nine," Coach finished, closing his scorebook. The rest of the Orioles glanced down at the end of the bench, where Gabe sat alone, looking pale and sweaty.

"God, it looks like he's gonna puke!" Hunter whispered.

"I don't think he threw a strike in warm-ups," Sammy said. "Mickey lost ten pounds jogging after all the balls Gabe threw over his head."

"He'll be fine," Corey said. "Gabe's a gamer."

Just then, Gabe stood, moaned softly, and clutched his stomach.

"This is it!" Hunter said. "Told you! The gamer's gonna hurl!"

But just as quickly, Gabe sat back down. A few seconds

later, with all eyes still on him, he rose again and lurched over to where Hunter sat.

Leaning over, Gabe grabbed his stomach again and made a low retching noise.

Hunter recoiled in horror.

"Ewww! Gross!" Katelyn said, quickly scooting out of the way of the upcoming spew.

Just then Gabe smiled and straightened up.

"Listen, you little dork," he hissed at Hunter. "I am *not* going to hurl. But if I ever do, I'm going to make sure I hurl all over your fancy new spikes and that two-hundred-dollar glove your mommy bought you. And you better not make an error with that stupid glove today, either. Understand?"

For emphasis, he poked Hunter in the chest. Hunter turned red as the rest of the Orioles cracked up and chanted: "GABE! GABE! GABE!"

It broke the tension. By the time Coach called them together again, the Orioles were ready to play ball.

"All right, let's do this," Coach said. "I think it's safe to say we're all a little wired, right? So let's just concentrate on playing sound, fundamental baseball. Gabe's gonna pitch lights-out, so just field your positions the way you always do and we'll be fine.

"At the plate, don't try to kill the ball," he continued. "Just meet it and drive it. If we do that, we'll score some runs. Okay, hands in the middle. Ready? Orioles on three."

"One, two, three . . . Orioles!" they shouted. Seconds later, they sprinted onto the field under a Carolina-blue sky as their families cheered wildly and the PA announcer intoned: "FOLKS, HOW 'BOUT A BIG HAND FOR THE DULANEY ORIOLES!"

As Coach had predicted, Gabe had settled down and was throwing smoothly. He mowed the Cardinals down in order in the first inning, striking out the first two batters on fastballs and getting the number three hitter on a weak grounder to Justin at second base.

Out in center field, Corey couldn't stop smiling. He had never played on a field so gorgeous. It almost felt like a sin to kick up a blade of grass or leave a spike mark on the dazzling white chalk lines that radiated at perfect angles from both sides of home plate.

He looked to his right and left and saw that Spencer and Katelyn were smiling, too, even as Katelyn rocked back and forth on her toes, studying the batter with her usual laser-like focus.

When the Orioles were up, they discovered that the Delaware pitcher, a tall, long-armed kid with a herky-jerky delivery, was on top of his game, too. Hunter led off with a walk, but Katelyn bounced into a double play, and Sammy struck out to end the inning. As the pitcher walked off the mound, he stared in at the Orioles dugout, bobbing his head the whole time.

"Yeah, you're bad!" Katelyn shouted. "We're so-o-o scared!"

This earned a quick death look from Coach, who didn't tolerate trash-talking of any sort from his players.

"Wait till I go up against that skinny bat-faced creep next time," Katelyn muttered as she retrieved her glove. "He's toast."

"Bat-faced?" Sammy whispered to Corey as they took the field. "Where'd she get that one?"

Corey shrugged. "You don't want to know," he whispered back. "I can only imagine what she calls me."

It was still 0–0 in the bottom of the second when Mickey walked and Corey came to the plate. This is it, he thought, my first at-bat in a big-time tournament. He could feel his heart pounding in his chest as his name was announced and the crowd gave him a polite round of applause.

He dug in, took a couple of practice swings, then stepped out and took a deep breath. Forget the slump, he told himself. It's a new at-bat, new game, new venue. The thought somehow calmed him. So did gazing out at the pitcher and discovering that Katelyn was right: the kid *did* have a bat face. Well, sort of.

Corey fouled off a couple of pitches, then quickly worked the count to 2–2. On the next pitch, a low fastball, he reached down and hit a sharp line drive over the short stop's head. For an instant, as he broke from the batter's box, his spirits soared—until he saw that the Cardinals left fielder was perfectly positioned to make the catch.

Still, as he jogged back to the dugout, Corey decided he could definitely live with that at-bat. In fact, it had seemed like a major breakthrough. He had taken a short, compact swing and hit the ball hard, just as his dad always preached. Just what Coach always preached, too. Heck, it was probably better than his last ten at-bats combined back home.

Just then a voice from the stands bellowed: "C'MON, ORIOLES. GET YOUR HEADS OUT OF YOUR BUTTS! YOU SHOULD BE OWNING THIS GUY!"

Gee, Corey thought, I wonder who that could be?

He didn't need to look up.

Mr. Encouragement was in the house.

The Orioles failed to get anything going that inning. Spencer struck out, and Ethan hit a harmless fly ball down the right field line, which the Cardinals first baseman staggered under before finally making the catch.

But an inning later, the Orioles broke the game open with a two-run double by Sammy, walks to Mickey and Corey, and another two-run double by Spencer. Ethan followed with a walk, both runners moved up on a wild pitch, and then scored on Justin's seeing-eye base hit between first and second.

Just like that it was Orioles 6, Cardinals 0, and the O's dugout was rocking. A moment later, the Delaware coach called "Time!" and signaled for a relief pitcher. The bat-faced kid was done for the day.

Which was when they heard it: loud, angry voices coming from the stands. Everyone in the Cardinals infield stopped and stared. Sammy and a few of the other Orioles scrambled to the top step of the dugout to see what was happening.

When he sat back down, Sammy said quietly, "Dude, it's your dad."

His heart quickening and his stomach dropping, Corey bounded up the steps and looked to his right. There, in the top row of the bleachers, was Joe Maduro, shouting and wagging his finger in the face of a man wearing a Cardinals hat. A woman who may have been the man's wife was standing between the two, attempting to calm the wild-eyed stranger in the Orioles T-shirt.

Good luck with that plan, Corey thought. Mount St. Maduro is just starting to erupt.

He sat back down and pulled his cap low over his eyes so the rest of the Orioles couldn't see the tears forming.

Well, that didn't take long, he thought. First game of the tournament and Dad is already out of control.

He shook his head sadly. It was going to be a long, long week.

Corey said nothing to his dad on the short ride back to the hotel. But as soon as they were in their room, he slammed the door shut and threw his equipment bag on the floor. Then he let it out.

"Really, Dad? The first game? We win and you get into it with another parent?"

Joe Maduro plopped down on one of the beds and clasped his fingers behind his head.

"That guy was a total jerk," he muttered. "And his wife was no prize, either. You talk about a foghorn voice. You could hear that woman back in Baltimore."

He reached for the remote, but Corey snatched it away and tossed it on the other bed.

"No, we have to talk about this!" he said, his face inches from his dad's. "You are *not* going to do this to me again. Not here. No way."

He went over to the window and threw open the drapes. Twenty floors below, the Sand Dune's pool sparkled in the bright sunshine. The Orioles were supposed to meet there in twenty minutes for some downtime before dinner. But Corey was still so embarrassed he wasn't sure he'd go. Not unless I can bring Dad and drown him when no one's looking, he thought grimly. Okay, that's sick. But it's also kind of appealing right now.

"Don't you even want to hear what happened?" his dad asked.

"I *know* what happened!" Corey said angrily. "It's always the same thing. Either A, you yelled something nasty about the other team that ticked off that other dad. Or B, that other dad yelled something that wasn't nasty at all, but you took it the wrong way and got mad just the same."

His dad started to say something, but Corey cut him off. "Mom talked to you about this stuff! *I* talked to you about it, too. But nothing gets through to you. Nothing! You just go on making people want to crawl into a hole! People you claim to"—here Corey drew air quotes—"'love.'"

As it always did, the mention of Anita Maduro brought a sad look to his dad's face. Instantly Corey regretted what he'd said. A year after his mom's death, his dad was still grieving. It wasn't fair to bring her up just to make his dad feel as bad as Corey was feeling.

Then Corey remembered a warm summer evening two years ago at Eddie Murray Field, and all the anger at his dad returned.

That night, his mom's cancer was in remission. For the first time in months, she was feeling well enough to attend a game with his dad.

The Orioles were playing the Yankees, and Corey had

gotten off to a good start at the plate: 2-for-4, with a triple and an RBI to help the O's to a 2–0 lead. Each time he glanced over at his mom, he saw her looking back at him, her face radiating pride and happiness.

It had made him feel so good. But that feeling didn't last long—for either one of them.

In the fifth inning, the Orioles pitcher had walked three straight batters before giving up a bases-clearing triple to the Yankees cleanup hitter. When the inning finally ended with the Yankees ahead 3–2, Corey's dad—with his mortified wife looking on—began loudly berating the Orioles coach for leaving the pitcher in too long.

The other Orioles parents had sat there in embarrassed silence, especially the mom of the poor pitcher who'd just gotten rocked. And the next time Corey glanced over at his own mother, he saw her rushing out to the parking lot, wiping tears from her face.

Yep, Corey thought as he gazed at the pool below, that was another all-star psycho performance by good ol' Dad. Nice thing for Mom to see on one of the few days she could actually enjoy life again.

Corey turned to his father. Joe Maduro lay on the bed with his eyes closed. For a moment, Corey wondered if he'd actually fallen asleep.

"I'm sorry, buddy," his dad said finally in a soft voice. He sat up and swung his feet onto the floor. For a long time he stared at the carpet with his shoulders slumped and said nothing. When he looked up again, his face was a picture of anguish.

"I . . . I don't know what comes over me," he said. "I go to each game thinking, 'Just enjoy it. Keep your mouth shut.' Then something happens and . . ."

Corey nodded. He knew where this was going.

". . . I just lose it," his dad continued. "Like tonight, that Delaware pitcher's dad got hot just 'cause I booed his kid. Then one thing led to another and—"

"Wait! You *booed* his kid?"

"It was just a little booing," his dad said. "Just when you guys shelled him and their coach took him out. And, I don't know, I guess I called the kid a name, too."

"You called him a *name?*"

"Yeah. Think I called him a loser or something. . . ."

"You called him a *loser?*"

"I know, I know. . . ." his dad said softly, looking down again. "Not good."

Corey stared at his dad in disbelief and thought: Sure, Delaware's a tiny state. But it doesn't matter. Now I can never show my face there again. Even if we're just driving through on the way to New Jersey. With my luck, the pitcher's dad is a toll collector. And he'll recognize Dad and call the police and have us both locked up or something.

He shook his head sadly. What made the whole thing even sadder was that Corey knew how much his dad loved baseball. In fact, he was the main reason Corey loved the game so much. Joe Maduro had played center field for two years at Towson University before a knee injury cut his career short. Almost everything Corey knew about the game he'd learned from his dad.

He thought back to all those summer evenings when Joe Maduro had come home exhausted from a long day of work at the insurance company. How many times had Corey met him at the front door with two gloves and pleaded with his dad to play catch?

And how many times had Joe Maduro smiled wearily, tousled Corey's hair, and said, "Sure, buddy. Just let me change out of this monkey suit first."

A few minutes later, the two of them would be out in the backyard, his dad throwing grounders or towering fly balls, until it was so dark the fireflies came out and the ball was just a shadow in the night sky.

Back then his dad had constantly encouraged him. That Joe Maduro was a far cry from the impatient, hypercritical Joe Maduro of late. Still, Corey knew that he wouldn't be half the player he was without his dad's help. And he knew what a good man and father his dad was deep down.

But this wild-man act of his at games was really getting old. Not to mention super-embarrassing for a certain Orioles center fielder.

When Joe Maduro looked up again, his voice was scratchy and his eyes were red-rimmed.

"Will you give me another chance? Before you write me off as a hopeless nutcase of a dad?" he said. "I promise: no more scenes. I'm just going to sit there at games and cheer for my son. Not a word to the other team, honest. Your sainted mom will be proud."

He pretended to zip his mouth. Then he struck an angelic pose: hands clasped in prayer, eyes gazing up to the heavens.

He looked so goofy that Corey couldn't help smiling. Already he could feel his anger ebbing, as it always did whenever his dad offered a teary-eyed apology for being a jerk and vowed to reform.

"Okay, Dad," he said. "We're good. But no more craziness in the stands. We've got to put an end to this. Please? For my sake? And Mom's?"

"You got it!" his dad said, clapping his hands with delight. He stood and glanced at his watch. "Hey, aren't you supposed to meet the team at the pool?" he said. "Go change and I'll go down with you. Buy you an ice cream, too."

As he pulled on his swim trunks, Corey wondered nervously if anyone on the team would bring up his dad's behavior at the game. Katelyn was sure to do it at some point, but maybe he could ignore her.

Anyway, the thought of cooling off in a nice big, pool was too much to resist, no matter what the other kids said.

"Mom," he whispered, smiling to himself, "you know I was only kidding about wanting to drown Dad, right?"

Besides, he thought, how could you ever drown someone who's willing to buy you ice cream?

Justin stood frozen at the water's edge. It was a warm, sunny morning, and with their second tournament game scheduled for later that afternoon, Corey and a few of the Orioles were hitting the ocean for the first time.

But Justin wasn't moving.

"I . . . I can't go in," he said in a quavering voice.

The other boys turned and stared at him.

"Okay," Sammy said. "Obvious question. Why not?"

Justin shook his head and gazed out at the waves breaking lazily in long, uneven rows.

"No, I can't tell you," he said. "You'll just laugh."

Gabe walked back to him and put an arm around his shoulder. "Justin," he said soothingly, "we're your teammates. We're here for you, bro."

"Yeah," Sammy said. "No one's going to laugh. Now, what's the problem, little dude?"

Justin looked hesitantly from one face to another. "You promise you won't laugh?" he asked.

"Absolutely," Gabe said. "You can count on us."

"Would we ever let you down?" Sammy said.

"Okay," Justin said, dropping his voice. "The problem is, I'm afraid of sharks."

The other boys looked at one another. Seconds later, they all cracked up, Sammy and Gabe laughing so hard they toppled onto the sand, trying to catch their breath.

"You said you wouldn't laugh!" Justin cried.

"Of *course* we said we wouldn't laugh!" Gabe said. "But you can't ever believe a kid when he says that!"

"You're worried about *sharks*?" Mickey hooted. "That's the dumbest thing I ever heard!"

Justin's face turned red as the Orioles continued to snicker. Just then Katelyn went sprinting past them. She splashed into the surf, dove expertly under a crashing wave, then stood and squeezed the water from her long hair.

She waded back to the knot of Orioles around Justin, who was now looking even more terrified than before.

"What's his problem?" she asked.

"Sharks," Gabe said.

"Specifically, he's afraid he'll be eaten by one," Corey added.

Katelyn stared dubiously at Justin. "You're standing in two inches of water!" she said. "What kind of a shark is going to attack you there?"

"Oh, you'd be surprised," Gabe said, elbowing Sammy. "There are sharks now that'll just leap out of the water and fly through the air and attack you right on the beach."

"That's true," Sammy said with a straight face. "Especially when they're hungry. And you know what their favorite food is? People think it's seals or other fish or something. But it's not. It's scrawny twelve-year-old second basemen."

"Yeah, they love them," Gabe said. "They're considered a delicacy by your general shark population."

"Pitchers, shortstops, outfielders—sharks won't even look at them," Sammy continued. "But a tasty second baseman? Oh, they go crazy! They'll rip into them, start with the legs, move on to the upper torso, maybe save the rest for a light snack later on."

Justin shuddered as the rest of the Orioles cracked up again and exchanged fist bumps.

"You guys are so-o-o breathtakingly stupid," Katelyn said, rolling her eyes. She went over to Justin and grabbed him by the wrist.

"Nerd," she said, dragging him into the water, "don't be such a wuss."

"No . . . no, *wait!*" Justin said in a high-pitched voice, trying to dig his heels in the sand. But Katelyn had his arm in a vise grip and wouldn't let go. She pulled him into the water as the rest of the Orioles howled with laughter.

"Don't worry," she barked as she dragged Justin farther out. "If we see a shark, I will personally kick its butt."

"She could do it, too," Corey murmured when Katelyn was out of earshot.

The other Orioles nodded solemnly.

"If it's Katelyn versus a shark, I'm betting on Katelyn every time," Sammy said.

The Orioles spent the next hour happily boogieboarding and bodysurfing as Coach and a few of their parents looked on from a small thicket of beach towels and umbrellas on the shore. Even Justin seemed to enjoy riding the waves after a while, once Katelyn showed him how, although he kept looking around nervously for a dorsal fin slicing through the water.

Unfortunately for him, this did not go unnoticed by the rest of the Orioles. At one point, Mickey swam underwater behind the jittery kid and pinched his leg, causing him to yelp and dash madly out of the surf. But upon seeing his teammates hooting and pretending to be sharks, complete with upraised hands on their heads in a lame imitation of a dorsal fin, Justin flashed an embarrassed grin and waded back in.

After the Orioles grew tired of swimming, they played touch football on the beach. When a long pass from Sammy sailed over his head into the water, Corey noticed the wind had kicked up and the surf was getting rougher now, the gray-green waves pounding the shore before flattening out in churning ribbons of white foam.

That's when he saw the boy.

He was only fifteen yards offshore, but Corey could see he was struggling. He was trying to swim toward the beach, but the current kept pushing him back as he thrashed helplessly. He looked frightened now, jerking his head back and forth as his arms churned through the water.

Corey shot a quick glance at the lifeguard chair, but it was empty. Then he remembered having heard the blast of a whistle moments earlier and seeing the lifeguard running to the other end of the beach to help another swimmer.

Without another thought, Corey sprinted into the surf and knifed under a big wave, trying to keep the boy in his sight as he surfaced. A half-dozen powerful strokes through the choppy water brought him near enough to see that the boy was about eight years old. His face was pale and he was gasping for breath.

Only when he reached the boy did Corey feel it: they were in a strong rip current. No wonder the kid was swimming as hard as he could and getting nowhere. They were drifting farther and farther from shore.

Suddenly the boy lunged at Corey and wrapped both arms around his neck, pulling them both under.

"Don't!" Corey sputtered when they surfaced. "You're choking me!"

He pried the boy's fingers apart and tried to remember what he'd learned in a basic lifesaving course last summer. Wasn't the first tip for dealing with riptides something like: don't panic?

Yeah, right.

So much for that tip, Corey thought. The kid's already losing it. And I'm not exactly feeling like a rock myself.

Now he remembered the other stuff he'd read about riptides: don't fight the current, you'll just get exhausted. Swim parallel to the shore until you reach calmer water. Only then turn back toward shore.

He hooked an arm around the boy's waist and began paddling sideways.

"Kick!" he shouted to the boy, who seemed to nod. Together they paddled and kicked furiously, slowly edging through the swirling water, which also looked muddy now, for some reason.

It seemed to take forever until Corey felt the current ease. He turned them toward land, making strokes with one arm and trying to keep the boy's head above water with the other, the waves propelling them forward.

Corey's shoulders had never ached so much. His legs felt like jelly, too, and his lungs burned. When they finally reached shallow water, he was too tired to climb to his feet.

He heard the sound of feet splashing toward them. Then someone was lifting the boy's other shoulder and dragging them both onto the beach.

Corey looked up to see who the helpful stranger was.

There was Katelyn, smiling down at them.

"Hang on, kid," she said to the boy. "I got you."

A woman who appeared to be the boy's mother came running toward them, her eyes wide with alarm. Right behind her were Coach, the rest of the Orioles, and their parents, all splashing into the water to help.

"Don't worry, everybody!" Katelyn shouted. "I saved him. He's going to be fine."

The Orioles watched in awe as the Cherry Hill Tigers whipped the ball around the infield in pregame warm-ups. The Tigers coach was hitting ridiculously hard ground balls and his infielders were looking like all-stars, making diving stops and tricky backhand picks and strong, accurate throws to first base.

What made it even more depressing was that every one of the Tigers was about six inches taller than most of the Orioles.

"That first baseman looks like he needs a shave," Mickey said in the quiet dugout.

"Check out the shortstop," Evan said, chomping nervously on his gum. "I think he drove the team bus."

"Two words: let's see their birth certificates," Hunter said.

The rest of the Orioles looked at each other and shook their heads.

"Uh, Hunter?" Sammy said. "That would be five words, not two."

"Is it the math that gives you problems?" Gabe asked. "Or the English?"

"Two words, five words, what's the difference?" Hunter said, waving his hand dismissively. "No way these guys are twelve years old."

Suddenly Katelyn leaped off the bench and slammed her glove on the floor, startling her teammates. She fixed them with a steely gaze.

"Who cares how old they are?" she shouted. "We're playing them—that's all that matters! Now quit all the whining! You're making me sick!"

As the other players looked down, chastened, Corey shook his head in wonder. Katelyn was without doubt the most brazen kid—boy or girl—he had ever encountered in his life.

He thought back again to the chaotic events of that morning. The Orioles were still buzzing about his daring rescue of the little kid in the rough surf.

But Katelyn's role was still being debated. The Orioles had watched the drama unfold from the beginning, from the moment Corey tore into the water after the floundering swimmer. But their parents and Coach had been unaware of what was happening until the end, when the frightened boy was dragged onto the beach by both Corey and Katelyn.

So in the eyes of the adults, both Corey and Katelyn were heroes, a conclusion the Orioles found laughable.

"She totally didn't do anything, dude," Sammy had snorted earlier as the team warmed up.

"Hung on the beach while you did all the work," Evan said.

"Yeah," Gabe said. "It's like in that Batman movie. What was it, *Dark Knight Rises*? Batman saves Gotham City from the evil terrorist Bane, right? But all along, Catwoman's taking credit for stuff. Trying to make Batman look like a punk."

Nevertheless, a reporter from a local newspaper, *The Islander*, had asked Corey and Katelyn to pose for photos and sit for a short interview about their ordeal. Corey wasn't surprised to hear Katelyn paint a glowing picture of herself selflessly churning through the rough seas to save the boy, because, as she'd added sweetly, "that's just the kind of person I am."

And the grateful parents of the boy had insisted on giving each of them a gift card with a generous balance to the Grand Slam merchandise shop, despite the fact that Katelyn had said modestly, "I don't deserve this. And Corey certainly doesn't, either."

Thinking back on it, Corey didn't consider himself a hero. He recalled how scared he'd been in the riptide, with the terrified kid clinging to his neck, threatening to drown them both. But Corey was proud of the way he had fought through his fear, kept his composure, and gotten the boy to safety. And he knew his dad was proud of him, too.

As soon as he and the boy had made it to the beach, Joe Maduro had wrapped him in a bear hug and said, "That was absolutely incredible, son! One of the bravest things I've ever seen! There's no doubt you saved that boy's life."

Maybe Corey would have cared more about the wild stories Katelyn was making up if he wasn't so worried about whether he'd ever get another hit and whether his dad would go crazy in the stands again and embarrass him.

Once the game began, the Orioles quickly discovered that the Tigers didn't just look good in the warm-ups— they *were* good. By the third inning, they led 5–0 on seven hits, including the hulking first baseman's two-run homer, which soared at least twenty feet beyond the Yankee Stadium fence.

"Told you he was a beast," Mickey said as the Tigers slugger finished his home-run trot. "I'm guessing he uses those Gillette Mach Three blades, just like my dad."

But Gabe was in no mood for jokes. By the end of the inning, he had the body language of a Death Row convict: head bowed, shoulders slumped, feet shuffling listlessly as he made his way to the dugout.

He fired his glove angrily against the wall and sat down. "Well, that sucked," he moaned. "I throw fastballs and they hit 'em. I throw curveballs and they hit 'em. I throw change-ups and—"

"Let me guess," Sammy interrupted. "They hit 'em?"

"Exactly," Gabe said, shaking his head mournfully.

The dugout was quiet for a moment. Then Katelyn chirped, "Hey, Vasquez, I have an idea. Why don't you try throwing something they *can't* hit?"

Corey leaped to his feet. He felt ready to explode. Sure, Gabe was having a rough outing. But he was a great pitcher, one of the best in the league. And he was going up against a tough team. To have one of his own teammates crack on him instead of encouraging him when he needed it most . . .

Corey was so livid his hands shook. He stomped over to Katelyn and was just about to say something when Coach came bounding down the steps.

"Hey, what's going on here?!" he said, glaring at the Orioles. "We're a team, aren't we? Only losers point fingers at each other when things aren't going well. I don't *ever* want to hear another player on this team criticize another player!

"If I do," he continued, "he or she"—he looked pointedly at Katelyn—"will be watching the rest of the tournament from the stands. Is that clear?" With that, he turned and jogged back to the third-base coaching box.

Corey was still steaming. He shot a murderous look at Katelyn, who stared back defiantly. Then he patted Gabe on the shoulder and in a loud voice said, "Keep battling, Gabe. We'll get some runs for you. This game isn't nearly over yet."

But the Orioles didn't get a runner on base until the fourth inning, when Katelyn led off with a walk against the second Tigers pitcher, a squat lefty with red hair, freckles, and a sneaky curveball.

"Here we go, Orioles!" Katelyn yelled as she tossed her bat aside. "No way Freckles is beating us with that junk!"

Sammy followed with a run-scoring double in the gap in left center, and Mickey walked, bringing Corey to the plate for the second time.

"C'mon, Maduro!" Katelyn shouted. "Big hit now! You're way overdue! Way, way overdue!"

Thanks, Katelyn, Corey thought as he dug in. Aren't you Little Miss Sunshine?

Corey let a fastball at the shins go by for ball one. Then the Tigers pitcher fooled him. He threw a big, looping curveball that looked like it would hit Corey in the shoulder. Corey bailed out, only to feel foolish when the ball broke sharply across the plate for strike one.

Oh, bet Dad loved that one, he thought grimly. Surprised he hasn't yelled anything about me being a little baby or something.

For an instant, Corey wondered if the silence from his dad meant his vow to change was actually holding this time. But now the pitcher was looking in for the sign and it was time for Corey to focus again, if he ever hoped to get out of this slump.

Go ahead, catcher, he thought. Put down two fingers. You know you want him to throw that big curve again. And he wants to throw it, too. I looked so lame on the last one, why wouldn't he throw it again?

The pitcher went into his windup. And here it came, another big, breaking ball, the stitches spinning wildly, the telltale sign. Corey read it the second it left the kid's hand. The pitch seemed headed for his batting helmet. Every instinct told him to duck, but he didn't.

Don't bail! Hang in, hang in! he told himself, and already the ball was starting to break down and in, just the way he had pictured it.

He waited another beat and whipped the bat around, catching the ball on the sweet spot and sending a shot down the left-field line. He saw Sammy heading for home and Mickey digging for third as the left fielder closed in on the ball. And now Corey's head was down and his arms were pumping as he rounded first and headed for second, sliding headfirst under the tag in a cloud of dust.

Tigers 5, Orioles 2. As Corey bounced up and brushed himself off, he couldn't stop smiling. It was his first hit in weeks, and now the Orioles dugout was alive. Even Katelyn was waving a towel and whooping on the top step. No outs, runners on second and third, Freckles frowning and nervously jiggling the resin bag.

It was a ball game again.

Corey glanced quickly in the stands for his dad, but he couldn't spot him.

No big deal, he thought. I know he's there somewhere. And I know he's smiling, too.

But the Orioles' comeback bid died after that. Spencer and Ethan struck out, and Justin hit a weak dribbler to the mound to end the inning. And in the sixth, Gabe, Hunter, and Katelyn went down in order to end the game.

Still, as the two teams lined up to shake hands, Corey found himself feeling better than he had in weeks.

Yes, the Orioles record in the tournament had dropped to 1–1. No one was happy about that. One more loss would probably kick them out of the championship bracket and into the consolation bracket.

But they had battled the Tigers for six innings. No one had quit, especially not Gabe, who had followed his rocky third inning by mowing the Tigers down in order before Danny relieved him.

The fact was, the Orioles had simply been beaten by a better team—and they knew it. There was definitely no disgrace in that.

Corey was heartened by how he had swung the bat, too. Sure, it was only a double to drive in a run. But after all his struggles at the plate recently, it felt as if he'd gone 4-for-4 with a pair of homers.

Best of all, his dad hadn't blown up at anyone. At least Corey hadn't heard any shouting or cursing in the stands to indicate a typical Joe Maduro meltdown. He looked around for his dad again and was surprised to see he was still nowhere to be found.

Suddenly there was a hand on his shoulder and a familiar voice said, "Somebody's bat's starting to heat up! You looked good out there, boy!"

Corey turned and saw Coach smiling and waiting for a fist bump.

"Thanks," Corey said. "Nice to do something to finally help this team. Only took forever."

Just then another voice cried, "HEY!"

They looked up to see Corey's dad waving at them as he hurried down the path from an adjacent field. He was wearing a backpack, which seemed strange.

"Where were you?" Corey asked when his dad reached them.

Joe Maduro grinned and gave them the thumbs-up sign.

"Scouting the team you play tomorrow," he said. "And guess what? You guys can't lose. Know why? 'Cause I know all their signs."

Coach's smile evaporated. Corey stared incredulously at his dad.

"You *stole* the other team's signs?" he asked.

"Well, I wouldn't say *stole*," his dad said. "Let's put it this way: they didn't exactly do a good job of hiding them."

"Joe, you shouldn't have . . . " Coach began.

But Corey's dad waved him off.

"No need to thank me, Mike," he said. "Happy to do it. Anyway, when the coach touches the bill of his cap, it means bunt. Hand across the chest means steal. Or maybe it's the other way around. But don't worry, I recorded everything."

He pulled the backpack from his shoulders and fished out a small video camera, which he held up triumphantly. He clicked the play button and footage of a kids' baseball game appeared on the screen, complete with various close-ups of players and coaches flashing signs.

Joe Maduro's voice provided the narration, sounding like one of those breathless documentaries on Animal Planet, where the guide is looking down at a herd of hippos bathing in a river and attempting to describe the scene:

"Scranton Blue Jays versus Allentown Yankees, July twenty-second. Okay, we begin with a tight close-up of the Scranton catcher. As you can clearly see, when he taps his right knee—*there!*—he's calling for a pitchout. Now watch this: the catcher waggles the mitt. See? That means he's going to throw down to first on a pickoff attempt.

"If we zoom in just a little bit more—*oh, that's a great shot!*—we see the catcher putting down one finger. Now he points to his left thigh—*right there!*—which means he's calling for a fastball inside and—"

"DAD!" Corey shouted. "Stop!"

"What?" his dad said. "Is it going too fast? Want me to slow it down?"

Corey looked at Coach in disbelief and shook his head.

"Joe," Coach said grimly, "listen to me, will you? When I said you shouldn't have, I really *meant* you shouldn't have. What you did is totally unethical. And illegal, too."

Now it was Joe Maduro's turn to look flabbergasted.

"Stealing signs?" he said. "People have been doing that since the beginning of baseball! Heck, the Cincinnati Reds said the Milwaukee Brewers were stealing each other's signs just last week. It was all over ESPN and in every newspaper in the country. What's the big deal?"

Coach closed his eyes and began massaging his temples with his index fingers, as if fending off a massive migraine.

"The big deal," he said wearily, "is that no matter how you cut it, stealing signs is a form of cheating. So what if they do it in the major leagues? Is that something we want to be teaching our kids? That the object is to win at all costs, even if it means doing something underhanded? Something even kids instinctively know is wrong?"

Joe Maduro looked at Corey, who nodded wordlessly.

"Sorry, Joe, I don't go for that stuff at all—no matter how you rationalize it," Coach continued. "I know some players and coaches do it at this level. But my teams don't. And they never will. I'm trying to teach these kids the right way to play the game. And the right way is by sharpening their skills and learning basic baseball strategy, not by putting their time and energy into stealing the other team's signs."

Corey's dad wore a dazed expression. Slowly, he reached down and clicked off the video camera. For several seconds, no one spoke.

"There's something else. . . ." Coach said finally.

Corey braced himself. Something in the tone of Coach's voice told him that whatever was coming wouldn't be good.

"Even if the Orioles don't look at this footage—which we won't—what you did may have gotten us in big trouble," Coach said. "Video-recording another team's signs is a huge no-no. Even at the major-league level, it's totally forbidden. If you don't believe me, look it up. If someone saw you doing it and reports it . . ." His voice trailed off.

The field was nearly deserted now, most of the Orioles having gone back to the hotel with their parents. Corey could see Mickey out in the parking lot, leaning against the family minivan, waiting patiently for his dad.

It was then that Corey noticed a burly man in a Scranton Blue Jays Windbreaker walking toward them. Accompanying him was a tall man in a white polo shirt with TOURNAMENT STAFF written over the breast pocket.

Neither seemed to be in a terrific mood.

"That's him!" the man in the Windbreaker said, pointing at Corey's dad. "That's the guy who was filming our signs!"

"Uh-oh," Joe Maduro murmured, quickly tucking the camera in his backpack. He turned to leave, but the man in the white polo blocked his path.

"Sir," the man said, "I'm Bud Jones, with the tournament. This is Art Davidson, coach of the Scranton team. Need to talk to you about this, please."

Seeing he was cornered, Joe Maduro turned defiant.

"I don't know what you're talking about," he said. "What makes you think I care about your stupid signs?"

"Oh, let's see," the coach said. "The fact you were leaning against the fence five feet away from me and pointing a camera every time I flashed the signs in the third-base coach's box—that was one clue. The fact that you were standing behind the center-field fence filming our catcher for two innings—that was another clue. Should I continue?"

Joe Maduro shook his head and looked down. Corey could see that all his bluster was gone. His shoulders were slumped and his normally tanned face was drained of color.

"Well, I'll continue anyway," the Blue Jays coach said. "The fact that you had the nerve to sit in the stands where all our parents could see you and play back what you recorded! What were you thinking there? And finally, the fact that we just saw you put a video camera in that backpack not even a minute ago."

The man shook his head in disgust. "Can I give you a piece of advice, buddy?" he continued. "Don't ever think of becoming a spy, okay? Because they'll catch you in about five seconds and march you in front of a firing squad."

Corey groaned and thought, Wish someone would march *me* in front of a firing squad right about now.

The man in the white polo shirt had been listening intently. Now he turned toward Coach and frowned.

"I'm going to have to report this," he said. "It's a serious violation of tournament rules. The rules committee will make the final determination. But as of right now, I'm afraid the Orioles are out of the tournament."

Corey spent the night tossing and turning, waking with a jolt from disturbing dreams the few times he actually managed to fall asleep. In one dream, he was at the plate with a 3–2 count and the pitcher delivered a fastball at least two feet outside. But when Corey tossed his bat aside and began trotting down to first base, the umpire yelled, "Stee-rike three!" And when the ump whipped off his mask, it turned out to be his dad, grinning like a gargoyle and cackling, "No free passes today, son!"

"How do you go back to sleep after something like that?" Corey muttered to himself, punching the pillow and trying to get comfortable again.

Early the next morning, he texted Sammy and the two slipped down to the pool, which was empty except for a teenage lifeguard busy flirting with pretty twin sisters.

They dove into the deep end. When they surfaced, Sammy gazed at the lifeguard with an annoyed expression.

"If I cramped up and sank to the bottom right now," he said, "how long would it take that guy to notice?"

Corey shrugged and didn't answer.

"I'm thinking twenty minutes, minimum," Sammy continued. "Maybe a half hour. By then I'd be so stiff, you could use my body as a coffee table."

"There's a cheerful thought," Corey said.

"I mean, *look* at him!" Sammy continued. "He's supposed to be protecting our lives, right? But he doesn't even know we're here! He's all wrapped up in Mary-Kate and Ashley Olsen over there."

Corey forced a weak smile, and Sammy finally caught on that his buddy was in no mood for jokes. They swam for a few more minutes before plopping down on a couple of lounge chairs.

"Look, dude, your dad didn't mean it," Sammy said quietly.

Corey nodded wearily. "I know," he said. "He feels terrible about the whole thing. He didn't get any sleep last night, either. Know what's even sadder? He still doesn't get it. He said we looked so bad against the Cherry Hill team that he thought we needed help in our next game. *His* help. Ha!"

The events of the past fifteen hours seemed like a blur to Corey now. After the confrontation with the Scranton Blue Jays coach and the lecture from the Grand Slam staffer, word had quickly spread—courtesy of Mickey's big mouth—that the Orioles had been booted from the tournament. Coach had then met quietly with the angry parents to explain the situation, a meeting his dad had wisely decided to skip, for fear of being turned into a human piñata.

As it was, Corey had spent the night expecting his hotel room to be stormed by a raging mob of moms and dads wielding pitchforks and flaming torches.

The rules committee was scheduled to render a final decision by eleven this morning on whether the Orioles were still in the tournament.

If the verdict was yes, they would play the Blue Jays at three that afternoon and live happily ever after. If the verdict was no, they'd be sullenly packing up and hitting the highway in a matter of hours, with an abashed Corey convinced that he'd have to wear a paper bag over his head for the rest of his life.

The way Corey saw it, only a miracle could keep the Orioles in the tournament now.

For one thing, the Blue Jays coach did not exactly seem like the type to forgive and forget his dad's transgression. For another, after doing some Internet research on his dad's iPad, Corey had confirmed that recording another team's signs was considered the ultimate sin at every level of organized baseball, especially at youth tournaments.

No, he thought, we're doomed. There's no point trying to be Mr. Optimistic about this one.

"If it makes you feel better," Sammy said, "everyone on the team understands this had nothing to do with you."

Just then, the gate opened and Katelyn appeared.

"Well," Sammy added, "*almost* everyone."

It was obvious that Katelyn was on a mission. She scanned the nearly deserted pool deck, her head swiveling back and forth like the point man on an infantry patrol. When she finally spotted them, her eyes narrowed and she made a beeline for Corey.

"What is the *deal* with your crazy dad?" she demanded. "And why can't you control him?"

"Good morning to you, too, Katelyn," Sammy said.

She shot him a withering look and turned back to Corey. "Your dad is killing us, Maduro," she continued. "Freakin' killing us! What's wrong with him?"

Corey jumped to his feet. He could feel his face getting hot. "There's nothing wrong with him!" he said. "He's a great dad! You couldn't have a better dad! He loves baseball. And he loves the Orioles! He's just a little . . . overinvolved."

"Seriously? A *little* overinvolved?" Katelyn said. "Ha! That's a good one! I heard all about that shouting match he had with the Dover Cardinals dad. And now we're on the verge of getting kicked out of here because someone gave him access to a video camera!"

Corey slumped back dejectedly in his chair.

"And look at the two of you," Katelyn said, shooting them a pitying look. "Doing nothing about the situation. Sitting there twiddling your thumbs like TweedleDumb and TweedleDumber."

"Oh, like you have a better idea?" Sammy asked.

"As a matter of fact, I do," she said.

She pulled up a chair and looked at them intently. "Here's what we're going to do, nerds," she continued. "We find out where this rules-committee meeting is. It's got to be around here someplace. And we show up there and plead our case directly."

"Ohhh-kay," Sammy said. "And what exactly *is* our case?"

"Simple," Katelyn said. "The bottom line is, we had nothing to do with this recording stuff. Nothing. It wasn't one of our players who did it. And it wasn't our coach. It was just one nutso parent"—she glared at Corey again—"who somehow decided that stealing another team's signs was a good thing to do.

"But our coach didn't look at the recording," she went on. "And neither did any of us players. No, we were as shocked as anyone at what this rogue dad did! So we look those committee members in the eye and we say, 'How can you kick little angels like us—straight-A students who love baseball, are wonderful to our parents, selflessly devoted to our brothers and sisters, et cetera—out of your tournament?'"

"Sure," Sammy said. "Like the committee's going to listen to a bunch of kids."

"Do you have a better plan, nerd?" Katelyn demanded. "No, let me rephrase that. Do you have *any* plan at all?"

Corey and Sammy looked at each other sheepishly and said nothing.

"Okay, then," Katelyn said, rising from her chair. "Go get everyone together. We'll meet in front of the hotel in an hour."

She started to leave, then stopped. "Oh, and tell everyone to wear their uniforms," she said. "We're gonna be a sea of orange at that meeting. A mighty sea of orange."

"'A mighty sea of orange?'" Sammy said when she was gone. "Where does she get this stuff?"

Corey shook his head and smiled. "I don't know," he said. "But it sounds pretty good about now."

Most of the Orioles were in front of the Sand Dune by ten thirty. They were met by a dejected-looking Katelyn, who sat slumped on the white marble steps as she punched numbers on her cell phone.

"I can't find out where the stupid meeting is!" she moaned. "I called the tournament hotline and no one answered. Good thing it's not a suicide hotline! Then I asked two Grand Slam officials I saw in the lobby, but they didn't know anything about a meeting."

"The mighty sea of orange might be drying up right here, dude," Sammy whispered to Corey.

Just then the hotel's revolving door swung open and Mickey emerged.

"Okay," he said, "the meeting's at the Grand Slam offices. It's just a five-minute walk up Coastal Highway." He pointed north. "We head in that direction."

"Wow, how'd you find that out?" Katelyn said, jumping to her feet. "That's amazing!"

"Yeah!" Evan said. "You're like that guy on *The Mentalist*! Using highly developed observational skills to deduce things. Or relying on paranormal mind-reading ability to obtain information."

"Uh, not exactly," Mickey said. "I just asked my dad. He's going to the meeting, too. He said he'd see us there."

It was another gorgeous North Carolina morning, with white, puffy clouds sailing across a brilliant blue sky. Nevertheless, the Orioles were in a somber mood. It was easy to sense how worried they were about the prospect of having a great week of baseball at a world-class facility cut short because of something they hadn't even been involved in.

Corey, on the other hand, was relieved that they were on the move and doing something—*anything*—that might help clean up the terrible mess his dad had made.

Joe Maduro had not been in the room when Corey returned from the pool. Corey guessed he had finally gotten so hungry he was willing to chance an encounter with an enraged, pitchfork-wielding Orioles parent, as long as he could also reach the McDonald's across the street.

On the other hand, Corey could also envision his dad getting tossed out of the McDonald's for berating the staff about not trying hard enough to make quality Quarter Pounders with cheese. Pushing that thought from his mind, Corey had scribbled a note to his dad explaining where the team was headed and promising that he'd be back soon.

The tournament offices turned out to be in a three-story brick building fronted by a courtyard with colorful flowers and lush tropical plants. In the lobby, the Orioles were met by a security guard.

"May I help you?" he asked. His name tag identified him as Sergeant Bowen.

"Sergeant, we are the Orioles," Katelyn said, sweeping her hand grandly to take in her teammates. "We demand to be let in to the rules-committee meeting that is deciding our fate. And I warn you: we are not to be trifled with."

"*Trifled with?*" Sammy whispered to Corey.

Corey shrugged. "Shhh. She's on a roll."

"We will not take no for an answer!" Katelyn continued, her voice soaring. "We will not be denied! No, sir, I assure you we will wait here all day to gain entrance if we have to! We will barricade ourselves here, we will go on a hunger strike, we will lock arms until the powers that be realize that—"

"Okay, go on in," Sergeant Bowen said pleasantly.

Katelyn was taken aback. "You mean . . . you're not stopping us?"

"Nope. Third door on the right," he said, pointing down a hallway. "No one's there yet. But make yourselves at home."

"Wow, you really showed *him*, Katelyn," Gabe said when they were out of the sergeant's earshot. The rest of the Orioles snickered as Katelyn flashed an embarrassed grin.

A moment later, they found themselves in a large conference room with soft beige carpeting and a massive mahogany table ringed by a dozen leather chairs. The Orioles clambered into the folding chairs set against one wall and waited restlessly for the meeting to begin.

At precisely eleven o'clock, five older men, all wearing Grand Slam blazers and serious expressions, entered the room. Each man nodded politely to the Orioles and took a seat at the table.

"We're doomed," Sammy murmured. "They look like the kind of guys who yell at you to get off their lawns."

"Or if your ball lands in their backyard," Gabe said, "they run their lawn mower over it before tossing it back."

The next to enter was Coach, who gave the team a quick wave as he sat at the conference table. Seeing him, Corey's heart sank. Coach was usually so positive and upbeat. But now he looked as if someone had just run over his dog.

The small, officious-looking man at the head of the table removed a folder from his briefcase. He slipped a pair of reading glasses low on his nose, folded his hands in front of him, and cleared his throat.

"My name is Mr. Meyers, and I'm the rules-committee chairman," he said. "We want to begin by acknowledging that the Orioles are here, obviously concerned about this hearing, and we welcome them." He managed a tight smile, as if the muscles in his face were unused to the effort. "Now let's get to the matter at hand."

Quickly, he summarized the case against the Orioles: A man in an Orioles cap was observed recording the Scranton Blue Jays' signs during their game. The man was discovered to be the parent of an Orioles player. When confronted with evidence of his wrongdoing, the man did not deny culpability. In addition—here Meyers shook his head sadly, looking pointedly at the Orioles—two witnesses reported seeing the man surreptitiously slip a video camera into his backpack.

"Coach Labriogla," he concluded, "it seems pretty cut-and-dried. I don't see how this committee has any choice but to dismiss the Orioles from the tournament. Do you have anything to say on behalf of your team?"

Coach rose to his feet. He rested his hands on the table for a moment and took a deep breath.

"Gentlemen, I know it looks bad," he said. "But you're only telling one side of the story."

Meyers arched an eyebrow. "There's more to this sordid little incident?"

Coach nodded. "Yes, one of our parents made a terrible mistake. And he's acknowledged that—well, sort of. But the fact is, no one on the team saw the video. I didn't watch it. And neither did any of my players. So no damage has been done."

"Oh, come now, Coach," Meyers said. "One of your parents comes to you with inside knowledge of an opponent's signs—a team you're about to face in a prestigious tournament—and you just wave your hands and say, 'No thanks, not a bit interested'? Is that what you expect this committee to believe?"

"I'm telling you the truth," Coach said with an edge to his voice. "I'll swear on a stack of Bibles if you want."

"That won't be necessary, Coach," Meyers said. "This is a rules-committee meeting, not a court of law. But I must tell you, what you're saying strains the bounds of credulity."

The room grew very still. Coach and Meyers stared at each other. Corey could see a vein pulsate on the side of Coach's neck.

He seemed about to say something. Instead, he sat down wearily. Meyers closed the folder in front of him with a satisfied look. "Well, then," he said, "if there's nothing else to discuss . . ."

"Yes, there is!" Corey heard himself blurt. In the next instant, he was on his feet. "Coach is telling the truth!"

Meyers gazed at him over his reading glasses. "And who might you be, sir?" he asked. The man's formality was chilling.

"I'm Corey Maduro." The words came out in a rush. "It was my dad who recorded the Blue Jays signs. But he never showed them to us! Coach wouldn't let him."

Sammy leaped to his feet, too. "Coach would never let us cheat! Like, a few weeks ago, he yelled at me for looking back at the catcher's signs when I was in the batter's box. He said if I ever did it again, I'd be off the team!"

"He did the same thing to me!" Gabe said. "One time I thought I picked up the other team's bunt sign. I went to tell Coach. And you know what he did? He put his hands over his ears and went like this: 'Blah, blah, blah, I can't hear you!'"

The rest of the Orioles cracked up. And they were relieved to see Coach laughing, too. But the outbursts seemed to startle Meyers. He shifted uneasily in his chair and looked at the other committee members.

"All right," he said. "I think we've heard enough. This committee will now meet privately to render its decision. If you'd all be kind enough to excuse us for a few minutes . . ."

The Orioles filed out into the hallway and gathered around Coach with worried frowns.

"Okay, we gave it our best shot," he said. "Now it's out of our hands. All we can do is hope for the best."

He looked at Corey, Sammy, and Gabe and said, "You guys were great in there. I'm really proud of all of you. I'm afraid I got a little rattled—couldn't think of anything else to say, and sort of gave up. Thanks for helping your ol' coach out."

Ten minutes later, Coach was summoned into the conference room. When the door opened again, Corey was so nervous he could feel his legs shaking.

But Coach was smiling! He gave them the thumbs-up sign.

"Let's get ready for the Blue Jays!" he said as the Orioles erupted in whoops and cheers.

Corey was so relieved that he slumped against the wall and closed his eyes for several seconds.

But the mood didn't last.

He opened his eyes to see Katelyn standing in front of him. She jabbed a finger in his chest.

"You're lucky, Maduro," she hissed. "Now keep an eye on your crazy dad. And make sure he doesn't screw this up for us again."

Lucky? Corey thought as he watched Katelyn stomp away. I've got a dad who turns into a howling maniac when he's around my baseball team and a teammate that can't stand me.

Yeah, just call me Mr. Lucky.

The taunting started as soon as the Orioles took the field.

"Cheaters!" cried a voice from the Blue Jays dugout.

"Where's your video camera?" another voice yelled.

"Hey, Orioles! Here's a news flash! We changed our signs!"

"You'd be pretty dumb if you didn't," Gabe muttered as he took his final warm-up throws before Mickey fired the ball down to Justin at second base.

Running out to right field, Katelyn made a point of cutting in front of Corey and glaring at him.

"Nice job, Maduro," she barked. "Because of your nutty dad, the natives are all stirred up. That'll really help our concentration."

Coach had warned the Orioles to expect a rough time from the Blue Jays and their fans, but the level of animosity still took them by surprise.

Not only were the Scranton players jeering at them, but their parents were as well. The two umpires had warned the Blue Jays about the name-calling before the game. But as soon as the parents joined in, the umps seemed disinclined to do anything more about it. And the Scranton coach stood impassively in the third-base coaching box with his arms crossed, seemingly oblivious to what his players were saying.

Corey glanced nervously up into the stands. Having his dad in the midst of such a tense atmosphere was like tossing a stick of dynamite into a broiling-hot warehouse. He was relieved to see his dad sitting as far as possible from both the Orioles' and Blue Jays' parents, in the bleachers down the third-base line. This self-imposed exile was a smart move, Corey thought. Unfortunately, it didn't guarantee that Joe Maduro wouldn't go thermonuclear if the abuse from the Scranton side continued.

As he had so many other times, Corey's dad had promised he'd be well behaved throughout the game. And he'd been visibly relieved when Corey burst into their hotel room with the news that the Orioles were still in the tournament and that his little video-recording stunt hadn't resulted in their banishment.

But in the next breath, his dad had made a point of saying, "Maybe now you guys will get your heads out of your butts and play some ball."

When Corey repeated the line to Sammy later, it quickly became a joke between the two.

"Can you even *play* with your head in your butt?" Corey asked.

"I don't see how that's physically possible," Sammy said. "Is that how the term *butthead* came about?"

"Then there's this," Corey said as the two dissolved in

laughter, "what if you pulled your head out of your butt and went oh-for-four and made a couple errors? Wouldn't you want to stick your head *back* in your butt?"

Now, seeing his dad chomping intensely on his gum and jiggling his legs, Corey was glad Joe Maduro wasn't mingling with the other grown-ups. Mr. Noah was about the only O's parent still talking to his dad—and that was probably only because he needed a ride back home. Earlier, during lunch in the hotel dining room, most of the other moms and dads had spent more time shooting Joe Maduro dirty looks than eating their meals.

As stressed as he was about his dad, Corey was happy to be playing baseball again. For one thing, they were in a beautiful park, Wrigley Field, complete with the famous ivy lining the outfield walls. Coach had made sure to explain the ground rules to the Orioles outfielders: if a batted ball shoots into the ivy and you can't find it, raise your hands and it's a ground-rule double. Otherwise it's a live ball.

Corey was also glad that Coach still had him in the number five spot in the batting order. He was definitely putting better swings on the ball, and Coach seemed to have more and more confidence in him.

Despite the blizzard of trash talk swirling around him, Gabe pitched well from the beginning, setting the Blue Jays down in order in the first two innings. It was still 0–0 in the bottom of the second when Mickey led off with a clean single up the middle, bringing Corey to the plate.

After the PA announcer introduced him, Corey took a few languid practice swings. The Blue Jays catcher, a big kid with thick, linebacker shoulders, stood and studied him.

"You're that kid, right?" the catcher said. "The kid whose dad stole our signs?"

Corey felt his stomach tighten, but he was determined to show that he wasn't afraid. He stepped out of the batter's box and nonchalantly tapped the dirt off his spikes.

"Yep, that's me," he said. "But I can't sign any autographs right now. Maybe after the game."

The catcher's eyes narrowed and he returned to his crouch. He pounded his mitt and flashed a few signs. The pitcher grinned and nodded. The grin seemed odd to Corey. Uh-oh, he thought. But the pitcher was already in his windup and now a fastball was on the way.

It was headed straight for Corey's chin.

He ducked and went down in a heap, the bat flying one way, his helmet another.

The catcher snickered. "Wow," he said, "that was close. Guess our pitcher doesn't have his best control today."

Corey got up quickly and dusted his uniform. As Coach howled in protest from the third-base coach's box, the umpire whipped off his mask. He pointed at the pitcher, then at the Blue Jays coach, who was standing on the top step of the dugout.

"Coach, that's a warning!" the umpire said. "If he throws at anyone again, he'll be ejected!"

"Wha-a-a-at?" the coach said innocently, drawing laughter from the Scranton parents. "The ball slipped out of his hand. Is that a crime now?"

Corey gritted his teeth and dug in again. He stole a

glance at the stands and was relieved to see that his dad was still there, although he was standing now and glowering at the Blue Jays coach.

Oh, yeah, the volcano is rumbling, Corey thought. In a game earlier in the season, when a pitcher had accidentally plunked Corey in the shoulder, his dad had come charging onto the field to confront the other coach. Hope we don't have another "Fun with Dad" moment here, Corey thought.

Now the Orioles were massed in the front of their dugout, banging their bats on the cement and cheering. Corey fouled off the next two pitches, then worked the count to 3–2. When the Jays pitcher tried to slip a fastball past him on the outer part of the plate, Corey went with the pitch and drilled a double down the right-field line that scored Mickey for a 1–0 Orioles lead.

On the mound, the pitcher kicked angrily at the dirt.

"THAT'S SHOWING HIM, COREY!" his dad shouted. "NEXT TIME, SMACK ONE OFF HIS HEAD!"

At this, the Scranton parents seemed to turn as one and stare in Joe Maduro's direction. Hoo boy, Corey thought. Dial it down, Dad. It was nice to be hitting well again, but not if it caused an in-game riot.

Spencer followed with a single to center to score Corey before the Scranton pitcher settled down and got the next three batters to end the inning. Still, the Orioles were up 2–0. And Corey could sense they had gotten some of their confidence back after that less-than-welcoming reception.

"Great at-bat, dude," Sammy said as they trotted out to the field. "Hear that?"

Corey stopped. He cocked his head and listened. "I don't hear anything," he said.

Sammy nodded happily. "Right," he said. "That's the whole point. You shut those jerky Blue Jays up. And their parents, too."

But the Blue Jays quickly came back with two runs the following inning to tie the score. Danny relieved Gabe in the fourth. But it was still 2–2 in the top of the sixth when, with two outs, Danny surrendered a walk.

The Blue Jays erupted in chants of "ROB-BEE! ROB-BEE!" as their big catcher sauntered to the plate.

"Cleanup hitter!" Coach shouted to his outfielders. "Move back!"

Spencer, Corey, and Katelyn all took a few steps back. But Coach waved at them to move back even more.

"Who does Coach think this guy is, Matt Wieters?" Spencer said as they backed up again.

But on the very first pitch, the Blue Jays slugger sent a long drive slicing into the gap in right-center field. The ball took two bounces and skipped into the ivy. Corey and Katelyn converged on the spot at the same time.

Right away, Corey saw a speck of white in all the green. There it was! Maybe he could hold the base runner to a single.

But when he reached into the ivy, he saw it wasn't a ball at all. It was the scrap of an old towel. Frantically, he rooted around for the baseball.

"Hold your hands up!" Katelyn shouted.

But now Corey's right hand was stuck. The sleeve of his jersey was caught on something. It was a nail in the wall behind the ivy. Finally, he managed to tear it free and held up both hands.

But it was too late. Two runs had scored. The Blue Jays led 4–2. Corey could see them celebrating wildly at home plate while their parents high-fived one another in the stands.

"Well, that was smooth, Maduro," Katelyn said drily. "What were you doing in there? It's not an Easter-egg hunt, you know."

Danny got the next batter on a bouncer to second base to end the inning, but the damage was done.

As he sprinted off the field, Corey could feel himself burning with embarrassment.

Nearing the dugout, he heard it: "C'MON, COREY, YOU'RE KILLING THIS TEAM! WHAT ARE YOU DOING OUT THERE?"

He looked up to see his dad scowling at him from one side of the backstop. In the next instant, Joe Maduro turned on his heel and stomped out to the parking lot.

The Orioles got a pair of base runners in their half of the sixth, but both were left stranded. And just like that, the game was over and the stunned Orioles were lining up to slap hands. Final score: Blue Jays 4, Orioles 2.

Now it was official. Forget the championship round. They were headed to the consolation bracket. With all the rest of the losers.

To Corey, it all felt like a bad dream. How could a game turn so quickly? And on a fluke play involving the stupid ivy!

As he gathered up his bat and glove and kicked off his

spikes, Corey thought, Should be a fun ride back to the hotel.

He tried to imagine what his dad's opening remark would be once they got in the car.

"ARE YOU BLIND?" would be a good guess.

"GET YOUR HEAD OUT OF YOUR BUTT!" was another. Only now it didn't seem nearly as funny.

Corey looked up at the sky. The sun was just beginning to dip over the tall palmetto trees beyond the outfield wall. He was glad the Orioles didn't have a game the next day. He needed a break from baseball.

"Mom," he whispered as he slung his equipment bag over his shoulder, "I could use a little help with Dad about now."

Danny went missing the next morning. Coach called the rest of the team together in the hotel lobby at a few minutes past ten to deliver the news.

"Mr. Connolly says he hasn't seen Danny since breakfast," Coach said. "He's got to be around here someplace. So let's all fan out and look for him." He fished into the pocket of his sweatpants for his car keys. "I'll drive around the complex. The rest of you search anywhere you think a kid would wander off to.

"Oh, almost forgot," Coach added as he turned to leave. "There was a report he was last seen near the big pond. But that's unconfirmed, people."

Once he was gone, the Orioles traded astonished looks.

"Are you thinking what I'm thinking?" Corey asked.

"Depends," Sammy said. "If you're thinking about a mean, hungry twelve-foot reptile that lives in that big pond and would devour our diminutive friend in a heartbeat, then, yeah, that's what I'm thinking."

"Freddy the Gator!" they shouted simultaneously, bolting for the door.

"Hey, where are you going?" asked Katelyn, who'd just arrived. But the rest of the team was already sprinting across the rear patio, headed for the ball fields in the distance and the muddy split of water that lay beyond.

A few minutes later, they stood gasping for breath in front of a low chain-link fence that surrounded the pond.

Even at this hour, the place looked spooky. A thin layer of marsh gas hung in the air. Occasionally, there was a rustling in the dense underbrush that spilled down to the water's edge. Corey thought he saw something floating just below the surface on the far side, but he told himself it might have been just a log.

A really big log.

With yellow eyes.

"Well, at least there's a fence around this thing," Sammy said. "That's good. Even if Danny was here, Freddy didn't get to him."

"Fences can be climbed," Spencer said pointedly.

The rest of the Orioles turned to look at him.

"Okay, Detective Dalton," Gabe said. "Why would Danny climb the fence when he knows there's a man-eating gator lurking on the other side?"

Spencer shrugged. "Well, he didn't have a great game yesterday, did he? Seemed pretty upset, didn't he? I'm just sayin'. . . ."

Sammy snorted. "Really, dude? You're saying maybe he wanted to end it all? Just 'cause he gave up a couple of hits? Puh-leeze!"

"And," Gabe said, "aren't there easier ways to do that

than being dragged underwater in the razor-sharp teeth of a humongous gator? And being drowned or chewed to pieces? Sorry, I don't think he looked *that* upset."

"Plus, if anyone had a bad game, it was me," Corey said. "I'm the one that cost us the win, not Danny. Maybe I should climb in there and feed myself to Freddy."

"Well, don't let us stop you, Maduro," a female voice said.

The Orioles spun around to find Katelyn smiling sweetly.

"In fact," she said to Corey, "after your little adventure in the ivy, jumping in there's probably the right thing to do."

The rest of the Orioles chuckled uneasily. But Corey was ready to explode.

It was bad enough that he had had to listen to his dad go on and on in the car about how he messed up that play, how he should have thrown up his hands right away and not taken a chance on finding a ball in the thick plant growth.

It had been a classic Joe Maduro meltdown, too, complete with a florid face, bulging veins in his neck, and lots of fist-banging on the dashboard for emphasis.

Initially, these postgame tirades reduced Corey to tears and bothered him for days. Now he was so used to them he simply shrugged them off and attributed them to his dad's personality.

"Your dad's just a little high-strung," his mom had always said. "He doesn't mean it. He just gets carried away." And it had only gotten worse since his mom died.

Fine. Corey knew he had a nutcase dad who would lose it whenever a kid—and not just Corey, *any* kid—didn't play the game up to his so-called high standards. But he wasn't about to take any more crap about blowing a play from Katelyn.

"Look, Katelyn," he said hotly, "I don't know what your problem is. But I'm sick of you running your big mouth and always—"

Just then they heard a piercing cry. It came from the direction of the pond.

They turned in time to see a violent thrashing in the water. There was a flash of color—it looked like orange, but it was hard to tell. Then the water seemed to churn like a mighty whirlpool for fifteen seconds until finally it stopped.

A few air bubbles gurgled lazily to the surface.

Then there was only silence.

"What . . . was . . . that?" Spencer whispered.

"Please," Gabe said in a hushed voice, "someone tell me Danny wasn't wearing his Orioles T-shirt."

"If any bones come floating up," Justin said, "I am *so* going to freak out."

For a long time, no one spoke as they stared at the pond. It was a picture of calm again, the water lapping gently against the banks. But the trees seemed even darker and more ominous than before.

Their reverie was broken by the beep of a car horn. They turned to see Coach pulling up in his black SUV.

There in the passenger seat, grinning wildly, was Danny. He waved and gave them the thumbs-up sign.

Coach rolled down the windows. "You'll never guess where I found him. He walked all the way over to the batting cages to get in a few swings. Gave us all a little scare, didn't he?"

"Oh, he certainly did," Katelyn said in an icy tone.

She walked around to the passenger side and leaned in the window. Then she reared back and punched Danny as hard as she could in the shoulder.

"Oww!" he cried. "What's that for?"

"Listen, you little nerd," she hissed. "If you ever go missing again, I will personally hunt you down, understand? And when I find you, I'll smack you so hard your kids will be born dizzy."

With that, she turned on her heel and started walking briskly back to the hotel.

Coach clapped and hooted with delight. The rest of the Orioles looked on in disbelief.

"*Your kids will be born dizzy*'?" Sammy said.

Corey shook his head as he watched her disappear down the road.

"At least she wasn't hammering *me* this time," he said. "And that's always a good thing."

The big waterslide at Gusher World was called the Drop of Doom. Standing at its base and squinting up at its summit, which almost seemed to touch the clouds, the Orioles could see why it had that name.

The Drop of Doom was seven stories high, for one thing. A nearby sign noted that riders could reach speeds of between forty and fifty miles per hour on the descent. Not only that, but riders would also hurtle for several seconds in total darkness inside a narrow plastic tube before being catapulted into the flume below.

"Let's see if I understand the concept here," Sammy said. "It's not enough that this ride will terrify everyone who's scared of heights. It'll also freak out anyone who's scared of the dark and has claustrophobia, too."

"Great," said Justin nervously. "I'd rather go back in the ocean and take my chances with the sharks. Or swim with Freddy the Gator. I'm outta here."

Gabe grabbed him by the arm as they watched a young couple drop into the gleaming silver slide and shoot downward. "Look at that guy and his girlfriend!" he said. "Don't they look like they're having fun?"

"Are you out of your mind?" Justin said. "Listen to that high-pitched screaming. And that's just the guy."

"C'mon," Corey said, "what's the worst that could happen?"

"Aside from death, you mean?" Justin said. "Oh, lemme see . . . concussion, whiplash, broken limbs, severe bruising, internal bleeding, possible heart attack. I'm sure I left something out."

"Dude," Gabe said, "twelve-year-olds don't have heart attacks."

Justin peered up at the slide again and sighed. "Trust me," he said, "if there's a way for a twelve-year-old to have a heart attack, I'll find it."

They watched in silence as a few more riders climbed onto the platform at the top and seemed to drop from the heavens. Finally Gabe clapped his hands and began peeling off his shirt.

"I'm doing it, dudes," he announced. "The Drop of Doom doesn't scare me. Anyone else coming? Or are the rest of you a bunch of sniveling girlie-men? Uh, no offense, Katelyn."

Katelyn shot him a look. "None taken, dorkface," she said. "I mean, why should I be offended that you just demeaned my entire gender with another of your hideous stereotypes—this one straight from the Paleozoic era?"

The rest of the Orioles said, "Ooooh," and pointed at Gabe, who threw his hands in the air and backed up, laughing.

"Whoa! Easy, girlfriend!" he said. "All I'm saying is, we need to stick together. So we should do this as a team. Go up as a team and—"

"Die as a team?" Justin murmured.

Gabe rolled his eyes. "No one's going to *die*, Justin," he said. "Now let's go. We're wasting valuable time." He put his hand out, palm down. "Are we doing this as a team or what?"

One by one, each Oriole put a hand in the middle and repeated, "Team."

Finally even Justin joined them. "One request: closed casket if anything goes wrong," he said, before throwing a clammy hand on top of the others.

Now there was only one hand missing. The rest of the Orioles looked at Katelyn, who crossed her arms and stared back at them defiantly.

"Awkward," Mickey murmured.

"Come on, Katelyn," Corey said. "Don't leave us hanging here."

"Yeah, right, Maduro," she said. "Like anything *you* say would influence me."

"Ooooh!" the Orioles said again.

The seconds went by slowly as the face-off continued.

"Oh, fine," Katelyn said at last, slapping her hand on the pile. "I'll go on the stupid Drop of Gloom or whatever it's called."

The rest of the Orioles laughed. Actually, Corey thought, it *will* be the Drop of Gloom now that Katelyn's going on it. The girl had been especially crabby this morning, ever since throwing that right hook at Danny for scaring them all to death. Danny's shoulder was now a vivid black-and-blue, earning him nonstop ragging from the rest of the Orioles from the moment they arrived at the water park.

It was a hot, humid Carolina afternoon, and the line for the Drop of Doom was long. The Orioles passed the time laughing and joking with one another and admiring the expansive views of the water park as they climbed higher and higher.

Justin, though, was growing even more apprehensive.

"Remind me again why we're doing this," he said, wringing his hands and looking down. "This is like paying a lot of money and waiting forever in line to fall off the roof of a building. It doesn't make any sense."

"Don't overthink it," Sammy said. "Just focus on the great memories you'll have when this is over."

"Yeah," Gabe said. "Just imagine the sensation when you drop forty vertical feet in four-point-five seconds. And the blood rushes to your head. And you almost pass out. And now your stomach is all tied up in knots until you just wanna—"

Justin's eyes bulged. He yelped and made a break for the stairs, but Gabe and Sammy blocked his way.

"Uh-uh, too late to back out now," Mickey said, grabbing the back of Justin's swim trunks and giving him a vicious wedgie in the process.

"JUST-IN! JUST-IN!" the rest of the Orioles chanted as the little second baseman squirmed in Mickey's grasp.

When they finally reached the top, a breeze seemed to come up out of nowhere, causing the narrow wooden structure that enclosed the stairs to creak and sway slightly. By now, Justin had turned an ominous shade of green. Most of the other Orioles had suddenly grown quiet, too, as they gazed down at the sparkling blue water far below.

From this height, Corey thought, it looks like a little kid's wading pool.

"Okay, it's showtime!" Gabe said. "Who's going to start us off? Who's going to be the daring guy or girl"—he smiled at Katelyn, who made a face—"to show the world what the Orioles are made of?

"Who's going to ride the Doom?" he continued, his voice rising. "Who's going to be the incredibly brave and rugged individual who'll go first and stare down this monster for the rest of us?"

Nine index fingers quickly pointed back at him.

"Okay, then," he said, nodding. "I see how this is going to work. But I'm good with it. It only makes sense that the smartest, most athletic, and best-looking person on the team should lead us. Absolutely."

As the rest of the Orioles made gagging sounds, Gabe nodded to the kid in the Gusher World T-shirt who was monitoring the ride. The kid motioned for him to go. An instant later, he was hurtling downward and yelling at the top of his lungs. It seemed to take forever, but finally the Orioles saw him shoot out of the tube and splash down. He swam to the side and waved happily up at them.

"See, Justin?" Corey said. "The kid's alive and well. Nothing to it."

"Right," Justin said, shivering. "Do me a favor, anyway. Have an ambulance on standby."

One by one, the Orioles followed Gabe down the Drop

ol Doom, laughing and whooping the whole way. Even a whimpering Justin eventually summoned the nerve to go down, thanks mainly to Mickey's unyielding grip on his waistband and a firm push.

Finally, Katelyn and Corey were the only two Orioles left. Corey had planned to go down right after Sammy, until Katelyn abruptly cut in front of him.

"Oh, please, after you," Corey said, more than a little ticked off.

But Katelyn didn't seem to hear him. It was her turn. She sat quickly and grabbed the railing at the top of the slide with both hands.

Five seconds went by. Then ten seconds. Still she didn't move. Instead, she sat as if frozen, staring down at the blue water as the rest of the Orioles gazed up at her.

"Katelyn?" Corey said.

There was no answer. She gripped the railing so hard her knuckles were white.

"Katelyn," he said again, louder this time, "are you all right?"

When she finally turned to him, her face was deathly pale. Twin drops of perspiration glided down her cheeks. Her legs were shaking.

Corey had never seen anyone look so terrified.

The kid in the Gusher World T-shirt unclipped the two-way radio from his belt, pushed a button, and barked, "This is Matt. Looks like we got a Code Orange up here on Doom. Activate the usual response team."

Corey looked at him questioningly.

"Code Orange," the kid repeated. "Means a freak-out. Happens all the time. Better than a Code Red, though."

Code Red? Corey wondered. But Katelyn was still frozen in a sitting position at the top of the slide. Her whole body was trembling. She ran her tongue lightly over her lips and appeared to be trying to say something, but the words wouldn't come.

Corey pushed past the kid with the radio and reached her side.

"It's okay," he said. He grabbed her gently by the shoulders and pulled her back from the slide's edge. He could feel her breath coming in quick, shallow gasps.

"Can you stand up?" he asked.

Katelyn looked like she didn't recognize him. Her eyes were dull and unfocused. It reminded him of a video he had just watched of a window washer who was paralyzed with fear while ascending the three-hundred-foot pitched glass roof of an aquarium somewhere in the Midwest.

A rescue team had been dispatched to bring back the frightened window washer. But when a local TV reporter attempted to interview the man once he was back on the ground, he was still in shock and hardly able to breathe, let alone speak.

Corey lifted one of Katelyn's arms and the Gusher World kid lifted the other. Slowly they got her to her feet. Her legs were shaking.

"Somebody will be up in a while to help her down," the kid said.

But Corey waved him off and said, "I got this."

The sooner he got Katelyn back on the ground, he thought, the better off she'd be. She still hadn't said a word, and her legs were unsteady as they shuffled their way to the stairs, Katelyn leaning heavily on his shoulder.

The long walk down seemed to take forever. They drew puzzled stares from the dozens of ride-goers on their way up. Katelyn seemed in a trance, eyes staring straight ahead the whole time.

"Oh my gosh! Did you see her face?" one girl whispered loudly to her friends.

"She looks like she's seen a ghost! Must have been one ugly ghost, too!" another said as they giggled and bounded up the stairs.

Suddenly Corey felt sorry for Katelyn, which quickly brought on another feeling: confusion. The girl had been a major pain to him for weeks. She had made him look bad at every turn. Not only that, but she'd made no secret of the fact that she basically hated his guts and hoped he would go away.

So why was he feeling sorry for her now?

Why was he helping her to make this trek? Why was he shooting dirty looks at the mean girls making fun of her as they passed? Corey wasn't sure. Was this what his mom had meant when she talked about having "conflicted feelings" for someone? You felt bad for them, but you wanted to kill them at the same time?

Maybe.

All Corey knew was that he'd never even seen Katelyn look nervous before, let alone scared. And seeing her so panic-stricken bothered him. It was almost as if she was a completely different kid now from the tough, sarcastic girl he had known a half hour ago.

And he didn't like this Katelyn 3.0 version at all.

Finally, some twenty minutes later, they reached the bottom level of stairs. As they emerged, squinting into the bright sunshine, Corey spotted another teen in a Gusher World T-shirt.

"Okay, they just came down," the kid said into his radio. "Cancel the Code Orange."

"Hey, can I ask you a question?" Corey said. "What's a Code Red?"

The kid frowned and shook his head. "You don't want to know," he said. "Let's just say they're doing a lot of screaming up there if it's a Code Red. Sometimes we practically have to peel 'em off the wall. And take 'em down on a stretcher."

Bet that's a fun time, Corey thought.

He glanced at Katelyn and was relieved to see that she had finally stopped trembling. The color in her face was starting to return, too. But she still hadn't said a word.

As they walked down the hill, they saw the rest of the Orioles running toward them. Quickly, Katelyn snatched her hand off Corey's shoulder.

"What was going on up there?" Gabe asked. "We were watching you guys the whole time."

"Yeah, looked like somebody couldn't handle it," Sammy said gleefully to Katelyn. "Like somebody got really, really scared."

Everyone stared at Katelyn, who looked down and said nothing.

"No, she wasn't scared," Corey heard himself blurt. "She just has a stomachache, that's all." He turned to her. "A really bad stomachache, right?"

Katelyn nodded, eyes still glued to the ground.

"Didn't look like a stomachache from down here," Mickey said. "Looked like a case of chicken-itis."

"And how come she's not talking?" Justin said suspiciously. "When she was dragging me into the ocean to be shark bait, she didn't shut up."

"Let me ask you something," Corey said, jabbing him in his scrawny chest. "Last time you had a stomachache, did you feel like talking?"

No one said anything as Corey gazed fiercely at the group.

"Okay," he said finally. "If you'll excuse us, we're going to find Katelyn's mom. She needs to go back to the hotel and lie down. Meet you back here in a few."

The knot of Orioles silently parted as Corey and Katelyn pushed through and continued down the hill. Corey shook his head and chuckled to himself. He had talked about Katelyn having a stomachache with such conviction that even he was starting to believe it. How crazy was that?

Oh, well, he thought, it was like his mom had always said: sometimes you have to tell a little white lie to spare someone's feelings.

A few minutes later, they spotted Katelyn's mother sitting at a table with Coach and a few of the other parents at an outdoor café, all of them sipping iced teas.

Katelyn started to run to them. Just before she reached the table, she turned and looked back at Corey. Then she appeared to mouth something.

With all the noise around him, the rock music blaring from the speakers and the water gushing and the sounds of hundreds of people splashing and laughing, Corey couldn't quite make out what she said.

But it almost sounded like: "Thanks."

Corey and Sammy leaned against the dugout railing and stared in wonder at the cars streaming into the parking lot. Thirty minutes before the Orioles' game with the Arlen Indians, an overflow crowd was already in place. All three grandstands around the Yankee Stadium replica field were packed with cheering, banner-waving Indians fans, and the two sets of auxiliary bleachers were filling up fast.

"What do they think this is, a One Direction concert?" Sammy said.

Corey shook his head. "I know the Indians are the hot-shot local team," he said, "but did each player bring, like, thirty-five family members?"

"Maybe there's not a whole lot to do in Arlen," Sammy said. "Or maybe they want to experience the thrill of seeing youth baseball at its best, courtesy of the mighty Orioles from the great state of Maryland."

"Yeah," Corey said, "that's probably it. Why didn't I think of that?"

Suddenly each boy felt a whack on his shoulder, and Katelyn materialized behind them.

"Truth is, the crowd's here to see me, nerds," she said, nodding with conviction. "And I plan to put on a show for them. I'm thinking three-for-four at the plate, a couple of bombs, two or three stolen bases—you know, the usual. Oh, plus another *SportsCenter*-worthy diving catch in right field."

Cackling, she picked up her glove, punched the pocket a few times, and ran out with Danny to loosen her arm.

"Still humble, still selfless, still all about the team," Sammy said. He pretended to dab an imaginary tear in each eye with his sleeve. "I get all choked up when I think how lucky I am to be her teammate."

Corey laughed. But the truth was, he was thrilled to see Katelyn back to being her old self, even if that meant dealing with an ego the size of the Chesapeake Bay.

At breakfast in the hotel that morning, the team had sat together to talk about the upcoming game, which felt like a big one despite the fact that they were out of the championship round now. Katelyn hadn't said a word about the incident atop the Drop of Doom, even though a few of the Orioles had kidded her about it and wondered aloud about her remarkable recovery.

Two glasses of orange juice, two glasses of milk, and three pancakes—wasn't that an incredible appetite for someone who had suffered from a terrible "stomachache" just fifteen hours earlier?

"Shut it, nerds," Katelyn had growled finally, ending that line of conversation.

Once or twice, Corey had looked up from his own breakfast to see her looking at him. Each time, she had quickly looked away with what seemed to be the hint of a smile. Well, he couldn't be sure it was a smile. But at least she hadn't given him her usual glare, like he was a fly walking across her maple syrup.

Suddenly there was a commotion behind them as Mickey clambered down the dugout steps carrying his catcher's gear, with Gabe trailing behind.

"Are we going to warm up or not?" the pitcher barked.

"Patience, my grumpy friend," Mickey said, dusting off part of the bench.

This was Mickey's usual ritual, and the Orioles were familiar with it. Carefully, he laid out his gear. When it was arranged just so, he began pulling on one piece after another with all the solemnity of a medieval knight preparing for battle.

"I put on my equipment from the bottom up," he explained to no one in particular. "Start with the shin guards, okay? There we go. Then we move to the chest protector, which is adjusted like so."

He tugged hard on one strap and pretended to gasp, as if all the air had been sucked out of him.

"Unbelievable," Gabe said. "The kid does play-by-play of himself putting on his gear."

"The protective cup is already in place, of course," Mickey continued. "Anyone want to check? Can't be taking any chances down there, if you know what I mean."

"You need a cup for your brain," Gabe said. "Sounds like that's been hit a few times, too."

Mickey ignored him and reached for his face mask.

"Finally," he intoned dramatically, "the intrepid catcher

for the Orioles puts on the single most important piece of equipment he has—at least if you're a drop-dead handsome hunk like Michael James Labriogla."

Gabe groaned. "That's it, I'm officially going to hurl. Can we warm up now, Mr. Hunk?"

"I suppose," Mickey said, adjusting his face mask and picking up his mitt. "But don't make me sweat too much. Don't want to mess up this killer hair."

When the Orioles took the field, Corey scanned the stands for his dad. He finally spotted him in the bleachers behind first base, surrounded by a loud contingent of Indians fans wearing eagle-feather headdresses and bright red face paint, and waving red pom-poms.

Corey groaned. Oh, this isn't good, he thought. This isn't good at all.

It wasn't good because Joe Maduro, Corey knew, was of the opinion that anyone who painted his or her face and showed up in a silly outfit to watch a ball game probably had a screw loose and should be beaten with sticks. And he wasn't shy about expressing this opinion to others.

How many times had his dad been watching a Baltimore Ravens football game on TV, only to start ranting and raving when the cameras showed a bunch of fat guys in the stands wearing capes and tights as well as beads, feathers, and plastic bird beaks?

As for the pom-poms the Indians fans were waving, Corey knew that if one of them accidentally grazed his dad, he'd react as if he'd just been Tasered.

No, his dad sitting next to a bunch of rabid fans in Sitting Bull warbonnets was another powder keg waiting to blow.

Not that Corey could do anything about it now except pray that his dad would keep his vow not to cause a scene.

Quickly it became apparent that this wasn't Gabe's day. He walked four, gave up four hits, and the Orioles trailed 4–0 after three innings.

In the dugout between innings, he was disconsolate. "I suck!" he announced loudly. "I don't know why Coach gives me the ball. I can't get it over the plate. I can't get anyone out. I couldn't get my own mother out, the way I was pitching."

"Well, at least you're not overreacting," Corey said.

"Yeah, way to be Mr. Positive," Sammy said. "It's really helping things."

Justin led off with a walk for the Orioles in the top of the fifth. As he trotted down to first base, Katelyn popped up from her seat on the bench and retrieved her bat. She strode to the end of the dugout and began taking practice swings, talking to herself the whole time.

"What are you doing?" Mickey said. "You're not up."

"Just getting ready, dorkface," she said without interrupting her swings. "This is our inning. I can feel it. And guess who's going to lead the lumber parade?"

The rest of the Orioles looked at one another and snickered.

"'Lead the lumber parade?'" Sammy whispered.

"I don't know," Corey said, "but she's not kidding. See the look on her face?"

Katelyn had stopped swinging and was studying the pitcher intently now as she chomped furiously on a wad of bubble gum.

Danny followed with a hard single to right, sending Justin to third. And when Hunter followed with a walk to load the bases, Katelyn was up.

Before sauntering to the plate, she peered into the dugout from the on-deck circle and said, "This one's going bye-bye, boys."

By now, none of the Orioles were laughing. As if on cue, they jumped off the bench and climbed to the top step, watching with growing excitement as Katelyn dug in against the Indians pitcher.

"You don't think she's actually going to hit a—" Gabe began.

"Shush," Mickey said. "This could be good."

It was.

The Indians pitcher, a skinny kid with a high leg kick and herky-jerky delivery, went into his windup and delivered a big, looping curveball that seemed to break from somewhere out by third base. Katelyn stood motionless at the plate until the last possible second.

Just as the ball dove in on her wrists, she flicked the bat and hit a long, soaring drive that landed twenty feet beyond the left-field wall.

Grand slam.

As the Orioles dugout erupted in cheers, Corey and Sammy stared at each other in astonishment. Then the whole team ran out to mob Katelyn as she crossed the plate.

It took a while for her to get there.

As Coach would say later, Katelyn's home-run trot could be measured with an hourglass. She jogged slowly around the bases with a big smile, making it a point to hit each bag precisely on the corner with her right foot. As she rounded third, she tossed her helmet in the air big-league-style before stomping on the plate and disappearing in the celebrating throng of Orioles.

Orioles 4, Indians 4.

"New ball game!" Coach shouted above the din.

Back in the dugout, Katelyn flopped at the end of the bench and accepted a fist bump from Gabe, whose depression had instantly disappeared.

"I can't believe you called that shot!" he said.

She shrugged and pulled off her batting gloves. "That's why I should have been in the Home Run Derby, nerds. It's like I always say: the big dog's gotta hunt."

Standing in the on-deck circle, Sammy looked at Corey and grinned. "Now that," he said, "was pure poetry."

Katelyn's grand slam seemed to energize the
Orioles and throw the Indians fans into a funk.

Sammy followed with a sharp single up the middle,
and Mickey drove him in with a double down the left field
line for a 5–4 Orioles lead. Corey ran the count to 2–2 and
belted a run-scoring double over the left fielder's head,
which prompted the Indians coach to practically sprint
out of the dugout to make a pitching change.

The new pitcher was a short, heavyset kid with a decent
fastball who quickly struck out Spencer and Ethan and got
Justin on a bouncer to third to end the inning.

Nevertheless, the Orioles were ecstatic. They led 6–4
and the Indians dugout was nearly silent. As they grabbed
their gloves to take the field, the Orioles could see the
Indians coach clapping and trying to rally his team with
a fiery pep talk. But it seemed to be falling on deaf ears.
Most of the players were slumped on the bench with their
chins in their hands.

Corey peeked out to the bleachers and saw that everyone sitting around his dad seemed pretty morose, too. There wasn't a pom-pom in sight. That's good, Corey thought. Because if the Orioles were losing, waving a pom-pom in his dad's face would be like waving a red cape in front of a bull.

But Joe Maduro seemed to be in a good mood, gazing around happily and even attempting to make small talk with some of the discouraged Indians fans.

Corey breathed a sigh of relief. *Crisis averted—at least for now.*

Before taking the field, the Orioles gathered on the mound to pump up Danny.

"Two more innings!" Sammy said, jabbing his glove in Danny's chest. "All you gotta do is hold 'em, bro."

Danny smiled and nodded.

"Don't be afraid to let 'em hit the ball, nerd," Katelyn said. "You don't need to mow them down. You got good fielders behind you."

Again, Danny nodded.

"Throw strikes," Mickey said. "We'll mix in a few curveballs, sure. Don't want to be predictable. But mainly you want to throw that fastball over the plate so we get out of here with a win, okay?"

Everyone continued to look at Danny, who was still nodding amiably.

"Can I ask you a question?" Sammy said. "Would it be possible for you to actually say something?"

Danny shrugged. "How can I say anything when you guys won't shut up?"

"Good point," Sammy said. "Meeting adjourned."

Whether the pep talk helped or not, the Orioles could see that Danny was dialed in. At the beginning of the season, Coach had given the pitchers orange-and-black T-shirts that read: WORK FAST. THROW STRIKES. CHANGE SPEEDS. Coach said that was the philosophy of Ray Miller, the former longtime pitching coach of the big-league Orioles, who knew more about the craft of pitching than any man alive. Now Danny was following his advice brilliantly. He struck out the first Indians hitter on four pitches and needed just five more to get the next two batters on soft fly balls to the infield.

"Look at this kid dealing out there," Coach said as the Orioles hustled off the field. Danny beamed as he traded high fives with the rest of the team.

"Not bad, nerd," Katelyn said. "But that was the easy part. Let's see if you can close it out now. Or are you gonna pull one of these?" She grabbed her throat with both hands and staggered around the dugout making loud gagging sounds.

"There she goes again, spreading good feelings everywhere," Gabe said, glaring at her.

"Just trying to keep it real for the boy," Katelyn said. She plopped on the bench and chirped at Gabe, "Pardon me if I don't live in your little fantasy world. I'm all about tough love, nerds."

"Yeah," Gabe said drily. "We can see that."

The Orioles failed to get anything going at the plate and took the field again in the bottom of the sixth, clinging to a 6–4 lead. They needed just three more outs for the win. But it wouldn't be easy.

"Top of the order's up!" Coach shouted as Danny completed his warm-up throws.

This time Danny ran into trouble immediately. The Indians leadoff batter promptly singled up the middle, and the next kid laid down a perfect sacrifice bunt, moving the runner to second.

One out, one on, and the Indians had the tying run coming to the plate. This was their number three hitter, too, a big kid with thick arms and shoulders who looked more like a football player than anything else.

Seeing the kid now made Corey nervous. The boy had yet to get a hit, but Corey had seen that he had a quick bat and a nice compact swing that hinted at all sorts of power. Not only that, but his head was right on the ball after every swing, too, the way it was supposed to be.

There was no doubt about it. This kid was a pure hitter.

If he ever connects, Corey thought. He took a few steps back. Danny's first pitch to the kid was low and outside for a ball. Still, Corey took a few more steps back.

"Hey, Maduro!" Katelyn shouted from right field. "Play any deeper and you'll be in another zip code."

But Corey just waved her off. This kid was trouble, you could tell.

Danny went into his windup again and Corey winced the instant the ball came out of the pitcher's hand. It was a belt-high fastball right down the middle of the plate— a room-service fastball, his dad called them, because the hitter didn't even have to work for it. It practically showed up at your bedside under a silver platter.

The big kid was ready for it. He picked his left foot up, almost imperceptibly, and lashed a line drive into the gap in deep left-center field.

Spencer turned and started back, but Corey could see he was playing too shallow to catch up to this one. Now Corey was off, running as hard as he could to his right. No way I get to this, he thought. But with a half-dozen long strides, he somehow closed in on the ball.

At the last second, he dove and reached out as far as he could. He felt the ball land in his glove with a soft *WHUMP!* and then he was crashing hard to the ground and skidding across the grass, his chin scraping the ground.

"Squeeze the ball, squeeze the ball," he kept telling himself. He held out his glove for the umpire to see, the ball peeking out from the top of the webbing in a classic "snow cone" catch.

But he didn't allow himself any time to revel in it. Quickly, he picked himself up and whirled around.

The runner on second had taken off on contact. Now he was rounding third base as the Indians coach waved frantically for him to go back.

The kid's feet seemed to spin in midair, like the Coyote in a Road Runner cartoon, before he put on the brakes and retraced his steps. He was fast, too, but Corey uncorked a strong throw to second. Justin stretched for it like a first baseman, with one foot on the bag, and he caught it just before the runner slid in headfirst.

"We got him!" Corey said, shooting a fist in the air.

Except . . . no.

The umpire was calling the kid safe!

Emphatically, too.

"Safe, safe, safe!" the ump shouted, scissoring his arms back and forth in front of him. As the Indians fans cheered, Coach shot out of the dugout to argue the call.

Only someone was already arguing it.

Corey would never forget the sight: an irate Joe Maduro, his face beet red and the veins in his neck bulging, pounding on the chain-link fence with both fists and howling, "NO-O-O-O!"

Then he hopped the fence and ran onto the field, wild-eyed and snarling, headed for the second base umpire.

Coach tried to intercept him, but Corey's dad just brushed him aside and continued to advance on the umpire. The ump, his eyes wide with alarm, backed up as two Sea Isle policemen sprinted onto the field, yelling, "Sir! Sir, stop! You can't be out here! Get back to your seat before—"

Corey squeezed his eyes shut. No, he thought, this can't be happening. Please tell me it isn't happening.

But it was.

When he looked again, things weren't any better. The policemen were escorting his dad from the field, one on each arm. The Indians fans were booing and hissing, waving, and making other rude gestures with their hands. The Orioles parents were standing and shaking their heads in disgust. And his teammates were looking on with stunned expressions, not quite sure what to make of the whole scene.

The rest of the game was a blur for Corey.

Danny got the next batter on a bouncer back to the mound, and the next batter struck out, and now the Orioles were winners, running their record to 2–2. But no one on the team was celebrating. They all lined up as if in shock to shake hands with the Indians.

"Nice catch," a couple of the Indians said as Corey went through the line. He was too numb to reply.

He ran into the dugout and slumped on the bench with his head down, cap pulled down low. He could feel the tears coming, and this time there was no way to stop them. He was dimly aware that Coach had sat down next to him and draped an arm around his shoulders, but it was several long minutes before Corey could stop sobbing.

As they gathered up their equipment, one by one the Orioles passed Corey and silently tapped him on the arm with their gloves.

Corey understood the message: Hang in there, dude. We feel your pain. We're with you all the way. Must suck to have a nutcase dad.

The last to come up to him was Katelyn. She squeezed his shoulder and bent down until her face was nearly level with his. Corey was startled to see tears in her eyes, too.

"Be strong, Corey," she whispered.

Later, he would realize it was the first time Katelyn had ever been nice to him.

In fact, it was the first time she had ever called him anything except Maduro.

Or nerd.

But right now he was too upset to care.

Right now it felt like the world was ending.

On the ride back to the hotel with Coach, Corey tried to picture the jail cell where his dad was being held.

Was it like what you saw in the movies and on TV, the gray steel bars, a thin mattress on a metal bunk bed, and a dirty toilet, where you had to go in front of everyone?

Was there a drunk sleeping it off in the next cell, or someone on drugs raging nonstop at the guards in a high, piercing voice?

Then he had the weirdest thought. He imagined the prisoners going around the room asking one another, "What are you in for?"

"Assault," one might say.

"Dealing drugs," another might say.

"Armed robbery," a third might say.

Finally they would get to his dad, who would have to admit, "I flipped out at my son's baseball game and went after the umpire."

Oh, the other prisoners would love that one. Corey chuckled mirthlessly at the idea. He was glad his mom wasn't around to be embarrassed by seeing her husband behind bars in a sleepy North Carolina resort town—over a baseball game, no less.

Once they arrived at the hotel, Coach insisted that Corey shower and change and then have dinner with him and Mickey. After dinner, Coach and Mr. Noah were going to head over to the police station to check on his dad.

It was around six when Corey went up to his room. He slid the key card in the lock and pushed the door open, only to find his dad sitting in a chair in the dimly lit room.

His dad jumped to his feet. "Corey . . ." he began.

Corey was shocked to see his father, and also relieved and angry at the same time. "Save it, Dad. Not interested. Not even a little bit."

He tossed his equipment bag on the bed, walked over to the curtains, and threw them open. "Okay, one thing," he said. "How'd you get out of the slammer?"

His dad's shoulders slumped and he stared down at the carpet. "I didn't get arrested, son," he said. "The police just talked to me. They let me off with a warning. But I was too embarrassed to come back to the field. I knew Coach would give you a ride." He shook his head sadly. "I couldn't face Coach again. Couldn't face the other parents, either. But mainly I couldn't face you."

Then his features seemed to harden. "But can I tell you something?" he asked, waving his hands in the air. "That umpire at second base was blind! I mean, he needed a cane! And a Seeing Eye dog! Here you make that great diving catch and that great throw—oh, I was so proud of you, son—and the runner's out by a mile, any fool can see that, and yet that stupid ump still—"

"Dad!"

Corey thought he was all cried out, yet he could feel the tears coming again. His hands were trembling. So many different emotions were hitting him at once.

And his dad still didn't get it.

Joe Maduro shrugged and dropped his arms helplessly to his sides. "I know, I know. . . ." he said.

"No," Corey said coldly, "I don't think you do. And you haven't for a long time."

He went over to the closet and pulled out his suitcase. He unzipped one of the side pockets and fished out some papers.

"Know what this is, Dad?" he asked, waving it in the air. "I read this post a few weeks ago, on a Web site for youth baseball. It's kind of the story of your life. It's got a great title, too. Want to hear it? It's called 'How to Tell if You're an Out-of-Control Sports Parent.'"

Joe Maduro winced and said nothing.

Corey sat down at the desk, smoothed out the paper with both hands, and began to read:

"'Number one: Parent screams instructions and criticism from the sidelines.' Sound like anyone we know, Dad?"

His dad continued to stare straight ahead.

"'Number two: Parent boos the other team or its coaches.' Oh, we definitely know someone like that! In fact, we met him at the very first game down here! 'Number three: Parent puts too much pressure on kid, emphasizing winning above all else.' Ha! I could write a book about a parent like that! Bet Mom could've, too."

His dad moaned softly. He started to say something, then stopped.

"All right," Corey continued, "now we're really getting to the good stuff. Are you ready? 'Number four: Parent yells at the referee or umpire.' And my new personal favorite, given the events of today, 'Number five: Parent runs onto the field during the game.'"

He was so upset now that his voice was starting to crack. But still he pressed on.

"You know, I think we could even add another one to the list. How about this? 'Number six: Parent almost gets arrested for interfering with the game, embarrassing the crap out of his kid and his kid's team and coach in the process.'"

In the next instant, he was sobbing again, his head down on the desk, the printout wrinkled and smudged beneath him. His dad ran over to hug him, but Corey pushed him away.

"You know I'd do anything for you, buddy," his dad said in a thick voice. "Anything. I'd lay down my life for you. I'd give you a kidney, I'd give you—"

Corey lifted his head. "You want to give me something, Dad?" he shouted. "Give me some space! Give me a dad I can be proud of! Give me a dad I don't have to worry about every time I look in the stands at one of my baseball games!"

He watched his dad's face crumple as he slumped dejectedly back in the chair.

Corey wiped his eyes with the back of his hands. For several minutes, the two of them sat in silence.

"None of this would have happened . . ." his dad muttered at last.

Corey looked at him quizzically. Was he going to blame this on his mom's death?

"None of this would have happened," his dad began again, "if that stupid umpire didn't blow that call."

Corey couldn't believe what he'd just heard. He grabbed his gear bag and ran for the door. He flung it open and sprinted toward the elevators. Punching the down button, he muttered, "Come on, come on, come on!" under his breath.

From down the hallway, he heard a door open and his dad yell, "Corey! Please! Come back!"

But he wasn't going back—not right now, anyway.

He had to get away.

It felt like he couldn't breathe.

It took more than twenty swings before Corey's hands stopped shaking and he could think clearly again. He watched another ball from the pitching machine shoot in on his wrists and quickly flicked the bat, sending a rocket up the middle that felt as if it would tear a hole in the net and keep going, maybe all the way back to Baltimore.

It's a wonder what a blowup with a crazy dad can do for your hitting, Corey thought. He was still working on pure adrenaline, having stormed out of the hotel and sprinted a half mile across the ball fields to the batting cages, his gear bag flapping against his hip.

There was no one else around. Dusk was beginning to set in, and a light ocean breeze had kicked up. To take his mind off his dad, he took to narrating his swings in the dramatic voice of a TV play-by-play announcer:

"Folks, that's a solid double down the left-field line! They can't get Maduro out tonight! They've tried every-thing: high heat, breaking balls, changeups. The kid is just wearing out every pitcher they throw out there!"

When you're hitting well, he thought, a batting cage

was about the best place in the whole world. You could lose yourself in the rhythm of the place, block out everything except the ball shooting from the long clear tube, the bat swinging in a smooth arc to meet it, and the familiar *PING!* of metal meeting horsehide.

If you took enough swings, you'd end up with sore hands, aching shoulders, and legs that felt rubbery from constantly striding into the pitch. But the pain was always worth it. There was no feeling more satisfying than meeting the ball just right and driving it.

It only went as far as the net, sure, but in your mind you were sending it to the farthest reaches of a packed stadium, and the poor outfielder chasing it had no chance of catching up to it, none at all.

"Three-and-two count now, two outs, bottom of the sixth . . ." Corey intoned. "We've got a tie ball game and it's all riding on Maduro's shoulders . . . here comes the pitch . . . and there's a drive to deep center field! The ballpark's not going to hold this one, folks! And it's . . . *GONE!*

"Unbelievable! Corey Maduro has done it again! A walk-off homer! You talk about clutch! How about this young phenom with the Dulaney Orioles!"

Now he cupped his hands around his mouth and added his own crowd roar: "AAARRRGGGGHHH!"

He heard the sound of clapping—only this was *real* clapping!

Then a voice cried out, "Yay, Corey!"

He spun around to see Katelyn sitting on the bench with her arms and legs crossed, looking on with an amused grin.

Corey's face flamed as he scowled and bent down to pick up some balls.

"Another hitting contest, Katelyn?" Corey said. "Is that what you're here for? You think you'll beat me this time? No thanks. Not in the mood. You're the winner, if that's what you want."

"No, that's not it," she said. She spread her arms wide. "Look, didn't even bring my bat."

Corey regarded her suspiciously. But he was in no frame of mind to play Twenty Questions, either. Thinking of that old game brought on a stab of pain. Twenty Questions had been his mom's favorite way to pass the time on family car trips when he was younger.

He turned back to the pitching machine and took a few more swings. But it was hard to concentrate with Katelyn sitting there silently behind him. He could feel her eyes boring into him, and it made him uncomfortable.

Actually, it was more than uncomfortable. It was kind of creepy.

"Don't you want to know why I'm here?" she asked finally.

Corey sighed and threw his bat down. He walked over to the water fountain and took a long drink.

"If it's to give me any crap about my dad, I don't want to hear it," he said. He furrowed his brow. "How did you even know I was here?"

"I saw you run out of the hotel," Katelyn said. "And you looked pretty upset. If I was upset, this is where I'd go, too. And it worked for Danny."

"Yeah, well, you don't look too upset to me," Corey barked. "So why *are* you here?"

That seemed to startle her.

"I . . . I just wanted you to know you're not the only kid with a parent who goes crazy at ball games," she said.

"Maybe," Corey said, plopping dejectedly on the other bench. "But I'm the only kid *here* with that problem."

"No, you're not," she said quietly. "Why do you think my dad never comes to our games?"

Corey looked up in time to see Katelyn frown. At that moment, he realized that he hadn't seen Mr. Morris even once this whole season. It was always Katelyn's mom sitting in the stands at their games, chatting with the other parents and cheering for her daughter and the team.

The only time Corey ever saw Mr. Morris was when he occasionally picked up Katelyn after a practice in the family's big, white minivan. And then he always seemed grumpy and in a hurry to get going.

"Okay, tell me about your dad," Corey said, his tone softer now.

"Long story," she said. "You probably don't want to hear it. Not after all the crap I gave you about your dad."

Corey shrugged. "I've got plenty of time. Trust me, I'm not going back to that hotel until I absolutely have to."

Katelyn took a deep breath and looked down at her hands. "My dad was just . . . *insane* at my games," she said. "Everything bothered him. He'd yell at our coach if I wasn't batting cleanup. If the coach told me to hold the bat a certain way, my dad would yell, 'Katelyn, what are you doing?

You're holding the bat too high!' As soon as I got on base, he'd start yelling for me to steal, even if the coach hadn't given me the steal sign. When I bunted, he'd yell at the coach, 'C'mon, let her swing away.'"

She shuddered at the memory.

"He had a voice like a loudspeaker, too. It was so embarrassing. I wanted to die. Thank God for my mom. She finally told him he couldn't come to my games anymore. And I told him if he ever did, I'd quit baseball. He could see I was serious."

"And he listened to you?" Corey asked.

Katelyn nodded. "Don't get me wrong—I love my dad. But it's his loss—that's the way I look at it. He doesn't get to see his daughter play a game she loves. A game she's pretty good at, too.

"Oh, my dad says he's changed," she continued. "He kept begging us to let him come watch me play this season. He wanted to come to this tournament. But my mom and I don't trust him yet. So now when we have a game, he stays home and watches my little brother. Which is its own form of torture, believe me. Because my little brother is a royal pain in the butt."

They both chuckled. Then Katelyn grew serious again.

"I guess that's why I gave you so much crap about your dad," Katelyn said. "'Cause he sounded so much like mine."

Corey nodded. "If my mom was alive, she'd tell my dad to stop coming to my games, too," he said. "But she died last year. And he won't listen to me. Now I'm thinking of quitting."

"No!" Katelyn said. The ferocity in her voice startled him. "I mean, you *can't* quit!" she went on. "You're too good. That catch you made today? That's the best catch I've ever seen a kid make."

Corey shook his head wearily. "Here we go, back to the sarcasm. You never stop, do you?"

"No, I'm *serious,*" Katelyn said. "You played that ball perfectly. I wouldn't have been able to make that catch in a million years. And then to get up after a diving catch, spin around, and make a perfect throw . . . that was unbelievable."

Corey jumped up and went over to the water fountain for another drink. This was all very confusing. He needed a moment to think.

"Can I ask you a question?" he said, sitting again. "Why are you suddenly saying all these nice things about me? Have aliens taken over your body? What happened to the old Katelyn who hated my guts?"

"I didn't hate you," she said softly. "I was just . . . jealous. Or envious. I can never get those two straight. I thought I deserved to play center field. And I was mad when Coach put you there and he stuck me in right field, where they put all the losers. I was mad at Coach, mad at you, mad at everyone on the team.

"But when you helped me at the water park . . . wow." She shivered again at the memory. "Anyway, I felt terrible about how I had treated you. And when you made that great play . . . well, you saved the game for us. And I knew Coach had made the right decision to put you in center."

"But what about *you*?" Corey said. "Talk about saving the game—you hit a freaking grand slam! And you called it beforehand, too! Remember all that 'big dog's gotta hunt' stuff?"

Katelyn waved her hand dismissively. "I know I'm good." She flashed him a smile. "My mom says I have an ego the size of the Washington Monument."

This sounded more like the Katelyn he knew.

"But you . . ." she continued. "You're better. Like I said, Coach made the right decision."

Corey sat in stunned silence. It was almost dark now. The moon was coming up, and off in the distance they could see lights winking on in the hotel windows.

Katelyn was waiting for him to say something. But his mind was racing and he felt totally tongue-tied. This seemed to happen a lot lately, especially when he was around girls, particularly smart girls like Katelyn, who seemed to be able to look at you and know what you were thinking.

So Corey did what he often did when he found himself in this predicament.

He changed the subject.

"I just thought of something," he said. "You still owe me an ice cream."

Katelyn seemed puzzled at first. Then it dawned on her and she smiled. "For the hitting contest, right?" she said. "Chocolate marshmallow cone, wasn't it?"

Corey nodded. "And not *just* chocolate marshmallow."

Now Katelyn burst out laughing. "I know, I know . . . with *sprinkles*," she said, standing. "Okay, let's go. If you move your slow butt, we can get there before the place closes."

Corey tossed his bat in his gear bag and smiled to

himself. It hadn't been the greatest day of his life. In many ways, it had been one of the strangest. And the problem with his dad wasn't going away anytime soon.

But this minute at least, things weren't terrible.

Not if there was ice cream in the immediate future.

The Orioles were practicing on one of the back fields at the complex, and Corey was absolutely killing it.

He had already made three circus catches in the outfield, drawing shouts of approval from Coach and high fives from his teammates on all three. And he had pounded the ball during batting practice, spraying line drives to all fields and even jacking two monster shots over the left-field fence.

Coach was rearing back and throwing some hard BP, too—there were no room-service fastballs on the menu today. This wasn't the Home Run Derby. Not only that, but he was also mixing in lots of breaking balls. Years ago, Coach had been an all-conference pitcher for Salisbury University on Maryland's Eastern Shore. And he still had a live arm—at least for "a fat old guy in his forties," as he put it.

Many of the Orioles were only too eager to bail out of the batter's box against Coach, especially when he whistled a high fastball under their chin or threw a slider that looked like it was about to plunk them on the shoulder before it broke off. But Corey was so locked in that it didn't matter what Coach threw—he was on it.

At the same time, though, he was still worried sick about his dad. The Orioles had one game left, tomorrow against the powerful Norfolk Red Sox. And all Corey could think about was what kind of horribly embarrassing move his dad would pull this time to leave Corey wanting to scream, put a paper bag over his head, and flee the state.

This morning, he had barely said two words to his dad before grabbing breakfast with the team and getting a ride to practice with Coach and Mickey.

After he had stormed out of the room, his dad had gone looking for him. Joe Maduro had searched everywhere: the pool, the hotel gym, the basketball courts—everywhere but the batting cages.

When Corey finally returned from having an ice cream with Katelyn, he'd found his dad pacing around their room, eager to explain himself. But Corey had waved him off and climbed into bed, leaving his dad sitting by the window, staring out at the night sky.

Now Corey was here at practice, still angry, but some-how looking like an all-star in every phase of the game. This was one of the true mysteries of his life: how it could be that the more worried he was about something, the better he played.

In the last few months of his mom's life, in the dark days when she was shuttling back and forth between home and the hospital to meet with grim-faced doctors and fight infections and get different treatments, Corey had played the best baseball of his life.

It didn't make sense—none of it did. He would show up for games with red-rimmed eyes, exhausted from not sleeping, so worried about his mom he could hardly think. But as soon as the first pitch was thrown, he'd somehow manage to block it all out and concentrate on what was happening between the lines, with great results.

The ball would jump off his bat. When he was playing the outfield, he'd study the batter intently and watch for the type of pitch being thrown, then get a great break on the ball no matter where it was hit.

Sure, the minute the game was over, all the worries and fears and worst-case scenarios about his mom and her illness would wash over him again. But at least for those six innings, he could escape.

Baseball would always do that for him. And it was doing it for him again now under the blue, cloudless North Carolina sky.

After batting practice, Corey reached into his gear bag for his glove when he saw it. There in the pocket was a note from his dad.

It was written on white notebook paper and read:

Corey,
I don't know what to say. Literally. I feel terrible. Your mother begged me years ago to get help for my temper, and I didn't do it. It was a big mistake, I see that now. But don't give up on me. I'm trying, even though I know it doesn't seem that way.
Love,
Dad

Corey shook his head and crumpled the note before firing it into a trash can. He was just starting to feel better. No way was he going to start thinking about all that again now.

Just then, Sammy sidled up to him with a puzzled look on his face. "You know that game What's Wrong with This Picture?" he asked.

"Sure," Corey said. "An all-time classic."

"Okay," Sammy said, "let's play it. What's wrong with *this* picture? Katelyn hasn't stopped smiling at you the whole time we've been out here. Every time you make a catch in the outfield, she's cheering like you're Adam Jones or something and you just climbed the wall to rob someone of a home run. Same thing during batting practice. 'Great hit, Corey! Way to drive the ball, Corey! You're really locked in today, Corey!' Dude, it made me want to hurl!"

Sammy shook his head in wonder. "Oh, and she keeps calling you Corey instead of Maduro. Or nerd. Which, by the way, is still the affectionate name she reserves for the rest of us. Although she likes to mix it up, too. Today she called me a dumb-ass when I forgot to cover second on one of her throws." He stared at his friend. "So what's the deal? Why has she suddenly morphed into the president of the Corey Maduro Fan Club?"

"Guess she came to her senses," Corey said, grinning. "She finally realized a kid like me is the total package: good looks, brains, charm, athletic ability . . ."

"Yeah, that must be it," Sammy said, rolling his eyes.

Suddenly he grabbed Corey's shoulders, spun him around, and got him in a headlock.

"If you don't tell me what's going on," he said, "I'll choke off your air supply. I can kill a man with these arms, you know. They should probably be registered as deadly weapons."

"Okay, okay," Corey said, laughing and throwing up his hands in surrender.

Quickly he recounted the events of the night before at the batting cage, including the conversation about Katelyn's out-of-control dad, her initial resentment of Corey playing center field, and her praise for his diving catch-and-throw against the Indians.

He told Sammy the main reason Katelyn was being nice to him—okay, maybe she was even going a little overboard—was probably that she felt sorry that he had a dad who was a whack job at games, too.

When he was done, Sammy whistled softly. "Seriously?" he said. "That is *so* not like Katelyn. Maybe it wasn't really her. You said it was almost dark, right? Maybe it was some other girl, a girl with an actual sweet personality. And you only *thought* it was Katelyn."

Corey chuckled. "No, it was her. She even bought me that ice cream she owed me."

"That does it!" Sammy cried. "Maybe you had a really high fever and you were seeing things."

A moment later, Coach called them together at first base.

"Probably don't need to tell you we have a tough game

tomorrow," he said. "The Norfolk Red Sox have two pitchers who hit close to seventy on the radar gun. So we might be slightly, uh, *limited* when it comes to offense."

"Great," Justin whispered a little too loudly. "We're doomed. All life is over."

"No, we are *not* doomed, Justin," Coach said, glaring at him. "But we need to maximize any scoring opportunities we get. So now we're going to work on baserunning drills."

The Orioles let out a collective groan. Baserunning drills were boring. They were all running and no fun— glorified wind sprints. It was the last thing they wanted to do in a gorgeous baseball setting like this.

What they really wanted to do was get back to the hotel, jump in the pool, and enjoy their last off day in Sea Isle.

"Okay, I can see you're all looking forward to this," Coach said, holding up his hands. "But if we get on base against the Red Sox, we're going to be looking to steal— every time. So I've brought along a friend who might be able to help us. In fact, some of you might recognize him."

Now the Orioles' jaws dropped. Walking toward them with a big smile was Nate McLouth, the undisputed stolen-base king of the big-league Baltimore Orioles. He was currently on the disabled list with a shoulder injury, which probably explained why he had enough free time for a trip to North Carolina.

"All right, let's get to work," he said. "Who's the fastest runner on the team?"

"Oh, that's easy!" Katelyn sang out. "It's Corey!"

The rest of the Orioles looked at her as if her head had just exploded.

"That's it," Sammy whispered to Corey. "I'm officially going to puke."

"Uh, no," Coach said quickly. "Actually it's *not* Corey. Hunter is our fastest runner."

"Fine," Katelyn said, pouting. "But Corey's probably the *second*-fastest."

Now Sammy made low, retching sounds until Corey elbowed him in the ribs.

"All right, Hunter, come here," Nate McLouth said.

He had Hunter drop into an athletic stance, knees bent, weight shifted slightly forward, and head up, to take a lead off first base. Then he went over how to break for second, how to explode to top speed during the first three steps, and how to slide into the bag at the best angle to avoid the tag.

For the next twenty minutes, the Orioles practiced the drill under McLouth's watchful eye. When he was satisfied with their progress, Coach brought them together again.

"Now we're going to work on a secret play," he said, rubbing his hands together.

A low murmur of excitement rippled through the Orioles. It made Corey chuckle. Nothing seemed to get young baseball players more fired up than the prospect of a secret play. It seemed as if every team in the country had a secret play, or was working on one.

In fact, there were so many secret plays out there

that Corey couldn't understand how they could be secret anymore. Especially since kid baseball players were the biggest blabbermouths in the whole world and loved telling everyone about the great secret play their team was working on.

And anyway, with twenty-nine other teams in the tournament, Corey wouldn't have been surprised if at least a dozen of them already had the same secret play in their playbook. But as long as the Norfolk Red Sox wasn't one of those teams, the Orioles might be able to make it work.

Coach had Gabe go to the pitcher's mound, Mickey get set up behind the plate, and Sammy take shortstop, each with their gloves.

"The Norfolk pitchers are pretty good, so it might be hard to steal on them," he said. "But that doesn't mean we can't steal on their catcher. Nate?"

McLouth nodded. "Okay, here's how it works." He told Hunter to take a lead off first base. "The pitcher throws a pitch, right? What you want to do is break for second the instant the catcher throws the ball back to the pitcher. Got that? Most catchers kind of lob the ball back to the pitcher. Some even stay in their crouches and lob the ball back.

"So if you get a good break," he continued, "you should be sliding into second base before the pitcher gets the ball and can whirl around to throw you out. Let's practice it."

Even with Gabe and Mickey knowing how the play worked, Hunter was easily able to steal second three times in a row. Gabe grew so frustrated he slammed his glove to the ground.

"That's cheating!" he cried. "And if it isn't cheating, it should be! That's not baseball, that's . . . *cheating!*"

"Not at all," McLouth said, chuckling. "That's smart, heads-up baserunning. You even see guys do it once in a while in the major leagues."

The Orioles were impressed with the play, nodding and fist-bumping one another.

"Okay, not every one of you is as fast as Hunter," Coach said. "But every player on this team should be able to pull it off if we call on you. It's more about getting a good lead and timing than about pure speed. And who knows who'll be on base when we need it?

"It's probably a play that's only going to work once," he continued. "After that, the catcher will practically walk the ball back to the pitcher to prevent a steal. But the one time it *does* work might win us the ball game."

Each of the Orioles took turns leading off first and practicing the play, with Gabe, Mickey, and Sammy rotating in as base runners, too. Twenty minutes later, practice was over.

"You guys are ready," Nate McLouth said, smiling again. "I can't stick around for tomorrow's game, but I'll get the play-by-play afterward from Coach. And I definitely want to hear if the secret play works."

He tipped his cap and the Orioles gave him a big round of applause. Then they began gathering up their equipment.

Making sure he was out of earshot of Katelyn, Sammy

draped an arm around Corey and said in a high-pitched voice, "Who's the fastest runner on the team? Oh, that's easy! It's COR-EE!"

"Shut up," Corey said, his face reddening.

But secretly he was thrilled to have Katelyn cheering for him instead of always making him look bad.

His dad was doing a good enough job at that.

Gabe stuck two fingers in his mouth and let loose a high, piercing whistle that echoed across the pond.

"Yo, Freddy!" he shouted. "Come out and play!"

"You're asking him to come out and *play*?" Sammy said incredulously. "He's an alligator, not a cocker spaniel. You want him to do tricks, too?"

The rest of the Orioles laughed. It was such a mild, sunny day that they had all decided to walk back to the hotel after practice. As they passed the muddy home of Freddy the Gator, they'd been drawn by loud, mysterious splashing sounds that died down as soon as they stopped to investigate.

Now they were all leaning against the chain-link fence, staring at the dark expanse of junglelike foliage and coffee-brown water.

Despite the warm sunshine, Corey felt a chill run through him. The whole place looked even spookier than the last time they were here. He could imagine all manner of creatures slithering and creeping and crawling through the trees and brush.

Not to mention the twelve-foot killing machine silently skimming somewhere through the murky water, huge jaws ratcheting in and out, razor-sharp teeth fixed in a crooked, scary smile as it stalked its next meal.

Or maybe it was simply sunning itself on one of the far banks, lying still as a rotting log, until it could snatch and devour some poor, unsuspecting woodland creature that ventured hesitantly into the swamplike ooze for a drink of water.

"Okay, I'm going to say something that might be very controversial," Ethan began.

"*You* and *controversial*," Katelyn said with a sneer. "Those are two words that absolutely don't go together. When I think of you, nerd, the first word that comes to mind is, oh, *boring.*"

Ethan ignored her and kept staring at the pond. "I don't think there's a big gator in there," he said finally. "In fact, I would be willing to bet all the money I have, which is seven dollars and forty-nine cents, that there isn't."

The rest of the Orioles turned to look at him.

"I don't think there's anything in that pond but a bunch of fish," he said, nodding with conviction. "And maybe some turtles and frogs."

"Oh?" Gabe said. "And what leads you to this stunning conclusion?"

"A few things," Ethan answered. "If there was a huge man-eating alligator in there, wouldn't there be signs all over the place?"

"Signs?" Sammy said.

"Warning signs," Ethan said. "Big signs that scream 'Danger! Killer Alligator on Premises! Do Not Approach!' Or something like that. You see any signs?"

"Dude, there's a fence around the place," Gabe said. "What's that for? To protect us from your killer fish and turtles and frogs?"

Ethan snorted and shook his head. "Look how low this fence is," he said. "Anyone could climb over it in five seconds. A six-year-old could hop this thing in a minute."

The Orioles looked at one another dubiously.

"Think about this, too," Ethan said. "How many teams are in this tournament? Thirty, right? How many kids is that?"

"You're looking at me?" Gabe said. "What am I, a human calculator?"

"Let's say it's more than three hundred kids," Ethan went on. "And they have ten or twelve tournaments here every year. How could they have all those kids walking around with a killer alligator lurking on the grounds?"

"He's not 'lurking on the grounds,'" Justin said anxiously. "He's lurking in that pond."

"No, he's not," Ethan said. "If there was a gator around here, the people who run this tournament would be opening themselves up to all sorts of liability issues."

"Liability issues," Gabe repeated, looking at the others.

"Let's go over a few," Ethan said. "Failure to keep grounds safely maintained—I think an alligator on the loose would qualify as unsafe, don't you? Failure to warn tournament participants of any hidden dangers. Inadequate supervision of a hazardous area. I could go on and on."

"Uh, no, that's okay," Sammy said. "Let me guess. Your dad's a lawyer, right?"

Ethan's eyes widened. "How did you know?"

"Lucky guess," Sammy said, rolling his eyes.

"With all due respect, counselor," Gabe said, "you're out of your mind. Look at this place! You don't think there's an alligator in there somewhere?"

Ethan didn't answer right away. Instead, he pulled his gear bag from around his shoulders and dramatically tossed it aside. He took off his cap and flung that aside, too.

Then he began climbing the fence.

"Not only don't I *think* there's an alligator in there," he said, "I *know* there's not. And I'll prove it."

The rest of the Orioles watched with stunned expressions. But before he could get halfway up, Katelyn tackled him and wrestled him to the ground.

"No, you don't!" she said. "I don't care how dumb you are. You're not committing suicide while I'm around. What, you get eaten by a crocodile, and I'm supposed to live with that the rest of my life? Or he just chomps off one of your legs and that's on my conscience forever? Uh-uh. Not gonna happen."

"Let me go!" Ethan yelled, struggling to free himself. "It's not suicide! There's nothing in there!"

"Shhhh, you're just having a little outbreak of stupidity," Katelyn said in a soothing voice while sitting on his chest and pinning his shoulders to the ground. "It should go away in a minute or two."

Just then they heard the sound of tires crunching on

gravel. A battered station wagon was coming down the road. When it skidded to a stop not far from them, a frail-looking old man in white overalls got out.

He nodded politely to the Orioles and opened the back door on the driver's side. Out jumped a little white terrier, wagging its tail and sniffing cautiously at the air.

The old man started walking around the fence, the little dog following happily. When the two got to the far side, the old man appeared to pull out a key and fumble with a pad-lock until a gate finally swung open.

"He's going in there!" Corey said in a hushed voice. "How can he go in there?"

"Because there's nothing in there!" Ethan squeaked from underneath Katelyn.

But the others ignored him.

"Maybe he's a professional gator wrestler," Mickey said. "I saw a show about those guys last month. They're crazy!"

Gabe shot him a look. "The man's like a hundred years old. He couldn't wrestle that little dog, never mind a gator."

"Whatever he is," said Katelyn, standing and pulling a disheveled Ethan to his feet, "that little dog will be Freddy's appetizer. And the old guy will be the entrée."

They watched the old man close the gate. Then he and the dog disappeared from sight behind a stand of high grass and cypress trees.

"If we hear a bloodcurdling scream," Justin said with a shiver, "I am *so* going to freak out."

Five minutes went by, then ten. Still there was no sign of the old man and his dog. Suddenly they heard a loud *thump* and saw a splash at the far end of the pond. Almost immediately, they heard the frenzied, high-pitched barking of the little dog.

The Orioles gasped and looked at one another.

"That's it, Freddy got the old man!" Justin cried. "And the dog is crazy with grief! Because he's lost his master, his best friend! Snatched by a monster that dates back to prehistoric times and pulled to a watery grave in those powerful jaws."

The others—all except Ethan—nodded solemnly.

Except . . . now they could see the old man and the little dog returning along the same path.

The old man was whistling as he closed and locked the gate. He picked up a stick and threw it ahead of him, and the little dog chased it.

When they neared the station wagon, the old man noticed the Orioles gaping at him.

"Something the matter, folks?" he asked.

"Aren't you afraid?" Mickey blurted.

The man looked surprised. "Afraid of what, son?" he said.

"Of the gator, of course!" Mickey said. "Freddy the Gator?"

"Oh, they got you with that story, too." The old man chuckled. "Yeah, at least a few teams always fall for that one. There's no gator in there, folks. We keep this area locked so no one wanders in. I'm just here to make sure the drainpipe isn't clogged. But the only creatures in that pond are a few trout and a few turtles. Far as I know, they can't kill you."

With that, the old man lifted the dog into the car and they drove off.

"I don't know," Justin said, staring after them. "Maybe turtles and trout can't kill you. But they could definitely mess you up."

Ethan picked up his gear bag and walked to the front of the group with a triumphant look.

"Hate to say I told you so," he said, "but I told you so. Now, I think all of you owe me an apology...."

Katelyn walked up and punched him hard in the shoulder. "Shut it, nerd," she said. "No one likes a know-it-all."

The Orioles were eating lunch in the hotel dining room when Mickey sat down with a meal of indeterminate origin smothered with ketchup and mustard.

"What . . . is *that*?" Gabe demanded.

"What?" Mickey said. "The thing on my plate?"

"No, the thing on top of your head," Gabe said. "Yes, of course on your plate! What *is* that?"

"It's a cheesesteak sandwich," Mickey said, picking up the gloppy mess with both hands and taking a huge bite.

Gabe regarded him suspiciously. "But there's something else going on there," he said. "What are those . . . *things* sticking out of it?"

Mickey opened the roll and peered inside. "Fries," he said, chewing furiously.

"You put *fries* in your cheesesteak sandwich?" Gabe said.

Mickey shrugged. "What's wrong with that?"

"What's wrong with that?!" Gabe repeated incredulously, looking at the others for support. "*Everything's* wrong with that! What *isn't* wrong with that? Who puts fries in a sandwich? That's like putting, I don't know, pizza in a sandwich."

"I wouldn't have a problem with that," Mickey said.

Now Katelyn stared at the sandwich and said, "Ewww, that is really, really gross! I can't even look at it!"

Mickey nodded happily and took another savage bite. It reminded Corey of a video he had seen recently of a great white shark tearing into a sea otter. Except the shark hadn't seemed quite as ravenous.

By now Mickey had vivid streaks of ketchup and mustard splattered all over his face, too, which was grossing out not just Katelyn, but the entire team.

"If you don't want to look at it," he said, waving the sandwich at Katelyn, "there are plenty of other tables where you can sit."

"Oooooh, you got owned!" the other Orioles cried as Katelyn shot Mickey a death stare.

Listening to all this, Corey managed a weak grin before listlessly picking at his food again. Even though it had been a hard practice and a long walk back from the pond, he still didn't have much of an appetite.

From the minute the Orioles returned to the hotel, all he'd been able to think about was his dad, who was holed up in their room with the curtains drawn, watching the Golf Channel.

Corey took this as a sure sign that he was still upset and depressed about the events of yesterday, because Joe Maduro didn't even play golf.

Corey didn't get golf, either. It looked incredibly boring, hitting a little white ball and walking after it, just to hit it again and walk after it again. Riding in a golf cart didn't look any more exciting, not unless you could put racing stripes on it, blow out the engine, and zoom around the course with your friends instead of playing the stupid game in the first place.

He was lost in thought, wondering if he should go back upstairs to talk to his dad, when he felt a tap on the shoulder.

It was Coach.

"Hey, if you're through with lunch, let's talk," he said. He found them a table in the back of the room, away from the others.

"Big game tomorrow," Coach said with a smile. "Last one of the tournament. But you look like you're ready. You sure came out of that slump, son. That was an all-world showing at practice today."

"Thanks," Corey said.

Normally, hearing praise like that from Coach would have thrilled him. In fact, normally it would have made him glow for hours, and he would have raced to tell his dad. But now he looked down and searched for something to say.

Coach leaned forward with his elbows on the table and his hands clasped in front of him. His expression grew serious. "Just had a long talk with your dad," he began. "I know you're worried about him. I'm worried about him, too. That's why I wanted to chat with you."

Corey braced for the worst. Coach had tried talking to his dad about his behavior at games a couple of times this season.

The first time, Joe Maduro had stomped away in a

cold fury. The next time, he had heard Coach out and even promised to change his ways. But by the next game, it was the same old story: he was a ticking time bomb in the stands, just waiting for the right moment to go off on another ump or parent or kid.

"First thing I got out of our conversation," Coach went on, "was how much your dad loves you. And how he wants only the best for you. He knows how hard it's been for you since your mom died. It's been hard for him, too. He's still hurting. Anyone can see that. Unfortunately, he's not dealing very well with being the only parent."

Corey sighed. "If he loves me so much, how come he keeps doing stuff like the other night? Running after the ump—I mean, that was the worst one of all."

Coach nodded sympathetically. "Right now it's obvious your dad can't control himself," he said. "But he's going to have to. I told him it's got to stop. I didn't pull any punches, Corey. I said this was it, that if he did one more thing to cause a disruption, I would have him banned from our games. And I will.

"I told him if he acts up at tomorrow's game, I'll have the police escort him off the field again. Only this time, I will personally press charges. Which means they'll slap the handcuffs on him and he'll be arrested."

Corey winced and fought back tears. His dad was all he had now. The idea of not having a family member in the stands during his games made him sad beyond belief. So did the idea of his dad being taken off to jail, and the thought of how horrible that would be for both of them.

"Anyway, I think that really shook him up," Coach

continued. "He apologized all over the place. He said he feels terrible for how he embarrassed you and the team yesterday. He says he really learned his lesson this time."

Corey rolled his eyes and looked away.

"I know, I know. . . ." Coach said. "You've heard all this before, right? So have I. I wasn't sold on him suddenly turning into a model citizen, either. Sometimes it takes a lot for adults to change behavior patterns they've had for years."

He leaned in closer and dropped his voice. "But I have an idea," he said. "It's something that might help us get through to your dad once and for all. Something that might really jolt him, show him how crazy he's been acting. I'm not one hundred percent sure it'll work. But I figure it's worth a try."

Corey was having a hard time seeing where this conversation was going. But at this point, he was willing to try anything. If Coach had an idea, it was better than anything rattling around in Corey's head right now.

"Okay, here's the plan," Coach said. "Your dad is coming to our room at seven o'clock tonight. He doesn't know why. All I told him was I had something I wanted him to see. Anyway, I'd like you to come with him. Would you do that?"

"I . . . I guess so," Corey said.

"Good man," Coach said. "We definitely need you there. I might have someone else there, too. A sort of mystery guest. But don't you worry about that."

Now Corey's curiosity was piqued. What did Coach have up his sleeve? He was one of the smartest men Corey had ever known. But his dad was the most stubborn man he'd ever known, a guy who seemed pretty much set in his ways.

Even worse, Joe Maduro seemed so clueless at times about how ridiculous his behavior seemed to everyone else.

Corey was about to ask for more details when Coach pushed back from the table and stood.

"Okay," he said, clapping Corey on the back. "See you at seven o'clock sharp. Keep your fingers crossed that this works. Who knows? But I have a good feeling about it."

With that, he signaled for Mickey and the two of them left.

It was all very mysterious, Corey thought. Mysterious and more than a little bizarre.

He went over to join the Orioles and saw Katelyn smiling up at him. She pulled out the chair next to her and said, "Sit here, buddy. I'm going for another chocolate milk—you want one? You must be whipped after that all-world practice you had."

Corey shot a quick glance at Sammy, who stuck his index finger in his mouth and pretended to gag.

Speaking of bizarre, Corey thought, the way Katelyn was acting definitely qualified.

At precisely seven o'clock, Joe Maduro
rapped sharply on the door to room 1511. Corey could see
that his dad was uneasy—it was written all over his face.
His dad didn't care much for surprises. And since he had
no idea what was awaiting him behind the closed door,
this qualified as a major surprise.

He'd already had his first surprise moments earlier,
when he'd told Corey he was going down to Coach's room
and Corey had announced he was going with him.

"Smile, Dad," Corey whispered now. "You look like
you're going to the electric chair."

His dad grunted. "Feels like I am. If they try to shave my
wrists and ankles, I'm outta here."

Just then, the door was flung open and Coach beckoned
them inside.

Mickey wasn't there. But in the dim light, Corey could
see there was another figure in the room. Sitting at a
corner table and sipping from a water bottle was the special mystery guest: Mr. Noah. He waved to Corey and rose
to shake hands with his dad.

Uh-oh, Corey thought, that's surprise number three tonight. One more and Dad might bolt back to the room for another marathon viewing session of the Golf Channel and four scintillating hours of how to fix your slice.

Coach nodded toward Mr. Noah and said, "I asked Barry to join us for a reason, which we'll get to in a minute. Hope you don't mind."

"I don't mind," Corey's dad said, looking around. He tried to muster a smile. "What's this all about?"

Coach didn't answer directly. "Take a seat over here, Joe," he said, pulling out a chair and placing it in front of the TV. A black cord snaked under the chair. The cord ran from a laptop on the bed to the flat-screen in the cabinet.

"Uh-oh," Joe Maduro joked nervously, looking at Corey, "it *is* the electric chair."

Coach laughed. "Not even close," he said as Corey and Mr. Noah plopped into the other chairs.

Coach stood before the three of them like a waiter about to introduce the day's specials.

"Okay, we're going to watch a video," he explained. "Barry shot this the other day, at my request. Sorry we don't have any soda or popcorn. And what do they always say in the movie theater? Please turn off your cell phones."

It was a lame joke, but they chuckled politely as Coach pushed the play button.

Instantly they could see it was footage of the Orioles' game against the Arlen Indians. Corey marveled at how clear the images were and how Mr. Noah had been able to zoom in on even faraway players and fans.

"Okay, let's get to the good stuff," Coach said, fast-forwarding furiously. "Actually, we really shouldn't call it 'good' stuff. Ah, here we are."

He hit another button and there it was all over again on the big flat-screen: bottom of the sixth, Orioles clinging to a 6–4 lead, one out, one on, and a kid built like a chimney with legs batting for the Indians.

They watched as the kid smacked Danny's fastball and Corey took off after it, arms pumping, legs churning, before making a diving stab in deep left-center and skidding half-way across the ballpark on the turf.

"Sweet!" his dad said softly. "That's one for the highlight reel." The other two men murmured in agreement.

Corey found himself suppressing a grin in the semi-darkness. It was weird watching yourself make a great play. He had never done it before. It almost seemed as if they were watching some other kid make that catch and rocket-throw to second base, a kid who looked like Corey and played like Corey, but wasn't really Corey.

Now the umpire was making the safe sign, making it over and over and over again to emphasize how sure he was that the base runner had gotten back in time. From the corner of his eye, Corey saw his dad stiffen in his chair. He heard him take a quick, short breath, too.

Joe Maduro knew what was coming next. Everyone in the room did.

It looked even worse on video.

The camera left the ump and swung dizzily to the left, where a wild-eyed man was shrieking and pounding the fence so hard you thought his fists would be reduced to raw, bloody stumps.

Then the man leaped the fence in a surprisingly athletic move for a big, middle-aged guy. He headed for the ump with a murderous look on his face. Corey had seen that look at his games, several times. It was a look that brought chills if you were on the wrong end of it.

Seeing it now, he felt sorry for the ump all over again. The poor guy must have thought he was about to take his final breaths on this earth.

Corey glanced at his dad again. Joe Maduro was wearing a pained expression, but his eyes were riveted on the video. Corey wasn't even sure if he had blinked yet.

The camera was still locked on his dad as he stiff-armed Coach to get to the ump and then was corralled by two beefy police officers and led off the field, the whole ballpark in an uproar.

Now the camera panned to Corey in center field, bent over at the waist, his hands on his knees, his glove at his feet, his head hanging low. It zoomed in and lingered for a good ten seconds until Corey slowly looked up, the picture of agony, tears beginning to form in his eyes.

"That's the shot I wanted Barry to get more than any other," Coach said quietly.

The camera left Corey and they saw more close-ups of each of the other Orioles in the field, watching with a mixture of shock and bewilderment as Joe Maduro was marched into the parking lot by the police.

Seeing his dad shuffle to the police cruiser on the video,

one cop holding each arm, Corey almost gasped. It looked like every "perp walk" he had ever seen on the six o'clock news, the bad guy being paraded in front of photographers and TV crews on his way to jail or court or wherever they were taking him.

The only thing that was different, Corey thought, was that his dad wasn't holding a raincoat over his head to shield his face, as so many of those perps did.

They watched Joe Maduro being placed in the back of the police car, the door slamming shut, and then the screen faded slowly to black.

When it was over, no one spoke at first.

Corey looked at his dad. He expected him to explode, but Joe Maduro sat there frozen, his eyes still locked on the blank screen.

"Anyone want to see it again?" Coach said.

Corey's dad slowly shook his head. He appeared to be in shock.

Coach snapped on the lights and went to the window to open the curtains. Mr. Noah brought his chair over and sat directly across from Corey's dad. Coach sat on the other side. Both men were now inches from his dad's face.

It reminded Corey of one of those reality TV shows about an intervention, where some poor person is confronted about his drug or alcohol problem and forced by family and friends to seek help.

"Nobody wants to humiliate you, Joe," Mr. Noah began in a soft voice. "That's not what this is about. But you had to see that video. You had to see how bad it looks when you go off like that. You had to see how embarrassing it is for the team and for Coach."

"But mostly," he continued, looking at Corey, "you had to see how much pain it causes your son, who doesn't deserve any of it."

Joe Maduro glanced at Corey with sad eyes, and quickly looked away.

"It has to stop, Joe," Coach said. "And one way or another, it will. Unfortunately, you wouldn't be the first parent banned from his kid's baseball games. You wouldn't be the first to be arrested for causing a disturbance at his kid's games. But if it happens again, I'll personally make sure that both those things happen. Do you understand?"

Joe Maduro looked down at his hands and sighed.

"It's just a baseball game, Joe," Mr. Noah said, his voice practically a whisper now. "Let the kids play it. Let them have fun. Except for Coach, the rest of us adults should just butt out."

When Mr. Noah was through, Joe Maduro reached over and patted Corey gently on the side of the face.

He smiled sadly. Then he rose and walked slowly to the door as if in a trance. They heard the door open. And without a word, he was gone.

Coach looked first at Corey, then at Mr. Noah. "Well, how do you think it went?"

Mr. Noah shrugged. "Hard to tell," he said.

Corey wasn't sure either. But he knew one thing. He had never seen that look on his dad's face before.

Never, ever.

The Camden Yards field looked like a freshly vacuumed green carpet under the bright stadium lights. It was the Orioles' last tournament game, and they were excited to finally play on their "home field." But after taking infield, they were puzzled to see not one, but two pitchers warming up on the sidelines for the Norfolk Red Sox.

Both seemed to be the same height and weight. Both had long curly brown hair spilling out of their caps. Both had the exact same delivery, too. Same smooth windup, same high leg kick, same graceful follow-through.

"Am I seeing double?" Sammy asked.

"Nope," Corey said. "That's Kyle and Kenny VanderMeer."

"Wonder if they're brothers?" Hunter said.

The rest of the Orioles turned and stared at him.

"What?" he asked.

"Seriously?" Katelyn said. "Nerd, is there something *wrong* with you? Like mentally?"

"Hunter, we're talking about two kids who look exactly alike and share the same last name," Gabe said. "Yeah, I'm pretty sure they're brothers."

"They could be cousins," Hunter said sullenly.

"What about the part where they look exactly alike?" Gabe said. "Wouldn't that seem to indicate that they're identical tw—"

"Cousins can look exactly alike," Hunter sniffed. "Well, sort of."

"*Sort of* exactly alike?" Katelyn said. She turned to Gabe. "Don't talk to him anymore. You're wasting your time. He's like the poster boy for dumb."

They went back to watching the VanderMeers warm up. The immediate impression was this: the brothers threw hard. Really hard. When either kid's fastball hit the catcher's mitt, it made a sound like the crack of a rifle. After about fifteen pitches each, both boys began snapping off what looked like killer curveballs, too.

Here was the weird part: One of the brothers was a right-hander. The other was a lefty.

"Please tell me there's not a *Kerry* VanderMeer warming up next," Justin muttered. "Who hits seventy on the radar gun. And is ambidextrous."

"That means he throws with either hand, Hunter," Katelyn said. "You'll learn that word if you ever make it to high school. Which I sincerely doubt."

Hunter scowled as the rest of the Orioles hooted. Corey shook his head. "No, from what I heard, there are only two VanderMeers."

Sammy turned to him. "Dude, how do you know so much about two brothers who pitch for a team in Virginia?"

"I'm embarrassed to tell you," Corey said.

"But you'll tell us anyway," Sammy said, wrapping his

hands around Corey's neck and pretending to strangle him. "Because if you don't . . ."

"Okay, okay," Corey said. "My dad told me about these two brothers. He checked out this team on some youth baseball Web site even before we left home."

"Cyber-scouting," Katelyn said, nodding. "Not good. My crazy dad used to do that, too. Drove me and my mom nuts."

Corey grinned. It would have been impossible to imagine two days ago, but he was actually beginning to like Katelyn. It was kind of her to tell him about her out-of-control dad—she didn't have to do it. Now here she was, bravely talking about her dad in front of the entire team.

It made him realize he wasn't alone, that there were other kids out there living with parents who could be obnoxious at times.

As for his own crazy dad . . . well, Corey wasn't sure what to expect from him today.

After last night's video intervention—or whatever that was in Coach's room—Corey had gone down to the hotel game room to hang out with the Orioles for a couple of hours. Coach had suggested it as a way of giving Joe Maduro some space, some time to think. By the time Corey returned to the room at ten, his dad was already asleep.

This morning, his dad had surprised him by joining him for breakfast, enduring the frosty looks of every Orioles parent except Mr. Noah. Joe Maduro hadn't said anything about the video on the car ride to the game, but Corey figured that was because Sammy and his dad had ridden with them, too.

One good sign: his dad hadn't seemed as tense on the ride over as he usually did before games.

Normally he'd be sitting rigidly in the driver's seat, with a death grip on the steering wheel while ticking off all the things Corey and the Orioles needed to do to win—plus all the things they'd been doing to screw up past games.

But today he'd spent the ride making small talk with Mr. Noah about the breakfast buffet.

The breakfast buffet! Corey had to laugh. Who would have ever believed that a pregame conversation with Joe Maduro could center on which was tastier, the sausage or the bacon?

"All right, everybody in here!" Coach said. "Last game of the tournament, people. Let's make it a good one. Maybe we're not playing for the championship, but we're playing for pride now. A win today makes us three-and-two down here. It's something we'll remember all summer."

He paused and said, "Oh, and don't forget, this game's being streamed live on the Internet."

Corey groaned silently. He had forgotten that little detail. That meant that if his dad did another high jump over the fence and another bull-rush of the umps, it would be seen not only by everyone here, but also by anyone watching back home—and all over the country, too.

Maybe all over the *world*, for that matter.

Great.

That was certainly something to look forward to.

When the Orioles took the field, Corey looked for his dad in the stands and was shocked to see him sitting with the other Orioles parents. Well, not exactly *with* them. He was sitting in the same bleachers, but four rows behind the other moms and dads. And sitting next to him was none other than Mr. Noah.

Good ol' Mr. Noah, Corey thought. Maybe he was hanging with Dad out of the goodness of his heart. Or maybe Coach had asked him keep an eye on the team's notorious parental loose cannon.

Whatever the reason, Corey was thrilled to see the two of them together. As a calming influence on his dad, Mr. Noah was better than a bottle of Maalox.

Gabe was throwing serious heat and he set the Red Sox down in order. When the Norfolk team took the field, it was Kenny VanderMeer, the lefty, who headed for the mound. His brother jogged out to center field.

"Okay, at least we know who we're facing now," Katelyn said, clapping. She turned to Hunter and said, "Start us off, nerd."

"Don't know if I can," Hunter said in a sulky voice. "I might be too dumb."

"Oh, did I hurt your feelings with what I said earlier?" she asked in a soft voice.

When he looked at her sadly and nodded, she punched him in the arm and snarled, "Too bad. If you don't get on base, nerd, I'm gonna hurt something else. Trust me."

"Now, that's a motivator," Sammy muttered. "It's like, 'Step up or I'll kill you.'"

But the Orioles didn't get anything going against the Red Sox until the fourth inning, when Katelyn drew a one-out walk, and Sammy followed with a weak flare that just made it over the second baseman's head.

Kenny VanderMeer looked ticked now. He picked up the resin bag and threw it down angrily before glaring at the second baseman.

"Look at this guy!" Gabe said. "Like he's all-world or something! Like he never gave up a hit before! Like he's not *supposed* to give up hits!"

"Like it was the kid at second's fault!" Katelyn said. "What a dork."

When Mickey walked to load the bases, the Norfolk coach called time and walked slowly to the mound for a conference.

Standing in the on-deck circle, Corey wondered if the Red Sox would bring the righty VanderMeer in to face him. You could almost see the wheels turning in the coach's head as he thought about the move. But finally he murmured some words of encouragement to his pitcher, smacked him on the butt, and walked back to the dugout.

Good, Corey thought. Leave him in. I can hit off this dude. No matter how good he thinks he is.

Lefties didn't scare Corey. Hard throwers didn't scare him, either. He was swinging the bat well again, and his confidence was soaring. Sure, if a pitcher threw hard *and* had a good breaking ball, he could wear you out, really make you look dumb.

But Corey knew there weren't too many twelve-year-olds who had both those things working for them.

Besides, the Orioles hadn't seen this VanderMeer throw a curve in the game yet. He was just pounding the strike zone with fastballs. Maybe he was one of those pitchers whose curve looks great in warm-ups. But when he throws it in a real game, someone smacks it into the next area code and the kid never throws another one.

So Corey was thinking fastball all the way as he dug in.

And that's what he got.

The first one was six inches outside for ball one. The second was low and away for ball two. Corey stepped out and beat back a smile. Two-and-oh. Hitter's count. If this next fastball was anywhere over the plate, he'd be raking.

The kid went into his windup and delivered. And here it came, right over the plate. Corey's eyes lit up.

Except . . . it wasn't another fastball at all!

It was a changeup.

Now alarm bells were clanging in Corey's head. He tried to check his swing—he was way out in front of the pitch. But it was too late. He hit a weak dribbler back to the pitcher, who quickly threw to the catcher to force Katelyn.

Corey ran as hard as he could down the line, but the catcher whipped a strong throw to first and got him by a half step.

Double play. Inning-ending double play.

Rally-killing double play, too.

The Orioles fans let out a collective groan.

As he trotted dejectedly back to the dugout, Corey stole a quick glance at the stands. Just then he saw his dad leap to his feet and cup his hands around his mouth. Mr. Noah jumped up, too, with a look of alarm as he watched Joe Maduro.

Corey braced himself.

Here it comes, he thought. Dad's about to unload on me. In a voice that can be heard in Montana.

All of it on streaming live freaking video, too.

They could hear it in Montana, maybe even in Mexico, too. That's how loud it was.

It cut through the crowd noise like a siren.

Only what came out of Joe Maduro's mouth wasn't anger at all.

It wasn't irritation and it wasn't impatience, or any of the other things Corey had heard in his dad's voice for months now whenever he didn't come through on the baseball field.

"GREAT HUSTLE, COREY!" his dad yelled. "THAT WAS A TOUGH PITCH! YOU'LL GET IT NEXT TIME!"

Corey was so shocked he stopped in his tracks. When he looked in the stands again, his dad was grinning and clapping like Corey had just smacked one over the fence. Standing next to him and also applauding like a madman was a relieved-looking Mr. Noah.

The other Orioles parents were turning around with bewildered looks, wondering what kind of alternate life-form had taken over Joe Maduro's body.

Everyone in the Orioles dugout heard Corey's dad, too.

When Corey reached the top step, Coach was waiting for him with a big smile and a fist bump. So was Sammy, who patted the top of his batting helmet, handed him his glove, and wordlessly trotted out to short. And Katelyn smacked him on the butt on her way to right field and said, "Bet hearing that was sweet!"

Corey couldn't get over how strange it all felt.

It was the first time in his baseball career that people looked happy to see him after he'd killed a scoring opportunity. But he understood what was going on. His coach and teammates knew what he'd been going through with his dad at these games. Now that Joe Maduro had just acted like a seminormal parent again, they were showing his kid some love.

The big question now was: How long would his dad's new persona last? Was this like Dr. Jekyll and Mr. Hyde? Would he go back to having a meltdown the first time an ump's call went against the Orioles?

But Corey had no time to think about that right now. His team was trying to win a ball game.

Danny came on in relief of Gabe and gave up a walk before striking out the next two batters and getting the fourth kid on a pop-up to Ethan to end the inning.

The score was still 0–0. The pitchers' duel continued. And it wasn't about to get any easier. Because strutting to the mound for the Red Sox was none other than Kyle VanderMeer, with a game face that would chill molten lava.

On his first warm-up throw, he uncorked a blazing fastball that sailed over the catcher's head and slammed into the backstop. As the catcher, a chunky kid with floppy shin guards, walked back to retrieve it, Kyle glared and shouted, "C'mon, c'mon, let's go!"

"Same great personality as his brother," Gabe observed.

"Must be fun to be around the two of them," Sammy said. "Like Christmas morning every day."

But Kyle VanderMeer turned out to be pretty good when the pitches actually counted. He struck out Spencer on three straight fastballs. Ethan managed to foul off a couple of pitches and run the count to 2–2, but he nearly corkscrewed himself into the ground swinging at a changeup for the second out.

Kyle was so confident now, he started overthrowing. Justin and Gabe drew back-to-back walks, giving the Orioles a flicker of hope. But Hunter barely took the bat off his shoulder, paralyzed by two fastballs on the outside corner and a curveball that seemed to break from somewhere out by the ocean.

"That curve was just *filthy*," he said as he waited for Katelyn to trot out with his glove. "How does that team ever lose a game with those two pitchers?"

Katelyn slammed the glove into his chest. Then she pointed to the scoreboard. "In case you haven't noticed, nerd, *they're* not in the championship game, either," she barked. "And they haven't won this one yet. We're right there with them. So quit your whining."

It was the top of the sixth, and before jogging out to their positions, the Orioles gathered around the mound to talk to Danny.

"We need three more outs from you," Sammy said. "Just

hold these guys. Give us a chance to win. Think you can do it?"

Danny nodded grimly.

"Do you *think* you can do it, or *know* you can do it?" Ethan asked. "There's a big difference."

"I *know* I can do it," Danny said, pounding his glove with his fist.

"Are you saying that because you think that's what we want to hear?" Justin asked. "Or do you really mean it?"

"Is this supposed to calm me down?" Danny said. "Or make me insane?"

"Yeah, is this really helpful?" Mickey said, pulling up his face mask. "It's not the *Dr. Phil* show. Why don't you guys leave him alone? Shoo!"

"Whoa! Leaving him, leaving him!" Sammy said, backing away with his hands in the air. "Excuse us for checking on the confidence level of a teammate."

Corey couldn't be sure, but as Danny warmed up, his fastball seemed to have gotten five miles per hour faster this inning. Maybe that's the key, he thought. We pester him, he gets annoyed, he throws harder.

Hopefully he gets batters out, too.

It worked that way with the first two Red Sox hitters. The first kid hit a two-hopper to Ethan for the easy put-out at first base. And the second batter hit a weak dribbler back to Danny for the second out.

That brought Kyle VanderMeer to the plate, lugging a big silver bat that gleamed under the lights. He took a couple of vicious practice swings and dug in to the batter's box. But just as Danny began his windup, Kyle held up one hand and asked for time.

Then he stepped out, reached into his back pocket, and made a big show of taking out a pack of bubble gum. He slowly unwrapped a piece and made another big show of sticking it in his mouth and chomping on it ferociously, all the while grinning cruelly at Danny.

Finally the umpire barked at him to get back in the batter's box.

"Un-freaking-believable!" Katelyn yelled to Corey. "Do you believe this kid? This could be one of the biggest dorks of our time!"

Danny was steaming, too. Corey watched him pace around the mound, shaking his head, as Kyle stalled. Big mistake, Corey thought. Danny was a little guy, but with a real live arm. Not the sort of pitcher you wanted to tick off before you stepped in against him, no matter how good a hitter you were.

Now Danny was amped.

He stared in at Mickey, got the sign, and blew a letter-high fastball past Kyle for strike one. His next fastball was belt-high, but Kyle was late on this swing, fouling it off into the screen in front of the Red Sox dugout.

Just like that, the count was 0-and-2.

Kyle stepped out again, wiped the sweat from his forehead, and tightened his batting gloves. But Corey could see he wasn't grinning anymore. Instead he was probably thinking: How does this skinny little kid with the matchstick legs throw that hard?

Now he dug in again, scowling and holding the bat high,

waving it menacingly in tiny circles. Danny threw him a curveball that was way outside. That's just a decoy, Corey thought. He's coming back with some major heat right now.

Danny rocked, kicked, and delivered. It was the hardest pitch he had thrown all night. The ball seemed to whistle on its way to the plate, darting and dancing the whole time. Kyle lunged forward, hands extended. But at the last second, he checked his swing.

The pitch flirted with the outside corner before it slammed into Mickey's mitt with a loud *WHAP!*

Now it was as if the entire ballpark held its breath.

"Give it to us, ump!" Corey whispered.

The umpire popped out of his crouch.

"STEE-RIKE THREE!" he shouted, pumping his right arm.

"NO-O-O!" Kyle shouted. "NO FREAKING WAY!"

He slammed the bat on the plate, kicking up a cloud of dust. Then he glared at the umpire before whipping off his helmet, firing it at the backstop, and stomping off to the dugout. When he was ten feet from the steps, he flung his bat against the far wall, scattering his teammates.

"The boy has a temper." Mickey chuckled as the Orioles hustled off the field.

"He certainly does," Coach said, frowning. "If that was one of my players, he'd be sitting—maybe for the rest of the season."

"More like for the rest of his career," Mickey muttered when his dad walked away.

The Orioles could see Kyle was still hot when he came back out to warm up. He was rearing back and firing as hard as he could on every throw, while shooting death stares at the ump, who pretended to ignore him.

"Make this guy throw strikes," Sammy said. "He's so rattled, he might be really wild out there."

"Good advice," Coach said. "All right, let's make something happen. This is it, bottom of the sixth. And everybody pay attention when I flash the signs. If we get a runner on, we might put on a certain play—if you know what I mean."

"*The secret play!*" Justin blurted as Coach jogged to the third-base coach's box. "Right? Isn't that what he's talking about? The secret play?"

Sammy punched him in the thigh. "Why don't you say it a little louder?" he hissed. "So their whole team hears it!"

Katelyn led off. "Need a base runner!" the Orioles cried as she strolled to the plate.

She turned and spit a shower of sunflower seeds into the air. "Consider it a done deal, nerds," she said.

As Kyle fumed silently on the mound, Katelyn took her time digging in, further infuriating the big kid.

When she was finally ready, she looked up.

And did something no one had ever seen at a baseball game before.

Katelyn smiled and waved at Kyle. It was a big, friendly wave, too, the kind you might give your best buds if you spotted them at the mall.

"Good luck, Kylie!" she yelled.

The kid's jaw dropped.

The Orioles were just as stunned as Kyle.

"Seriously? Did she just... *wave* to him?" Spencer asked.

"I think so," Mickey said. "Are you allowed to do that? Is waving legal in baseball?"

"What about calling him *Kylie?*" Gabe said. "That's wrong on so many levels that it *has* to be illegal."

"The ump's not saying anything," Corey said. "Guess it's okay."

Kyle's eyes narrowed and he growled, "Are you messing with me?"

But Katelyn kept smiling and the umpire quickly pointed at him and said, "Play ball!"

Kyle gritted his teeth and rubbed up the ball as he glared at Katelyn. Everyone in the ballpark knew what was coming next.

He went into his windup, reared back, and fired as hard as he could. Outside, ball one. The next pitch was even harder. Low, ball two. The third one sailed over the pudgy catcher's head for ball three.

"C'mon, Kyle, slow it down," the catcher implored. "Just throw strikes."

But Kyle just snarled and went into his windup again. And the next pitch was the hardest one of all, another low fastball that skipped in the dirt and ricocheted off the backstop, landing almost out near the mound again.

Katelyn tossed her bat aside and flashed a knowing look at the Orioles dugout. Then she jogged happily down to first base.

The Orioles had their base runner. They had a chance, and that was all they could ask for.

One run would win it now.

"That," Mickey said, shaking his head admiringly, "was an absolutely awesome at-bat!"

Kyle stomped around the mound, glowering at Katelyn and muttering to himself. The Red Sox coach quickly popped out of the dugout to try to settle down his pitcher. But with Sammy up, the Orioles could see that the big kid was still seething.

"Time for the secret play?" Justin asked. At least this time he had the sense to keep his voice low.

But Coach must have heard him anyway, because he turned to the dugout and nodded. He flashed the signs as Katelyn and Sammy studied him intently.

"Oh, God, I can't watch," Justin said, covering his eyes

with both hands. "Baseball makes me too nervous. I should've played lacrosse."

"Like that's less stressful," Gabe said. "People running at you full speed and whacking you with a stick every five seconds."

But Corey could see Gabe was not exactly the picture of calm, either. Not the way he was drumming his hands on his thighs.

The play worked perfectly. It worked just the way Nate McLouth said it would.

Sammy watched another Kyle fastball miss outside for ball one. And just as the catcher began to lob it back lazily, Katelyn took off.

"She's going!" the Red Sox infielders yelled. But Kyle was so startled he dropped the catcher's throw. By the time he picked up the ball and wheeled around, Katelyn was sliding into second with a stolen base.

Winning run in scoring position. The Orioles were on their feet and cheering. Kyle looked as if his head was about to explode.

"You can't get the ball back faster than that, fat boy?" he shouted at his catcher, who simply sighed, pulled down his face mask, and got back in his crouch.

"The boy's in full jerk mode," Gabe said, staring at Kyle. "Now's the time to get him."

But just then, Kyle seemed to compose himself. He took a deep breath and shook his head, as if he were shaking all the negative thoughts away. Then he toed the rubber again and calmly looked in for the sign.

Corey had seen this before with other good ballplayers he'd played with and against. They'd get mad, maybe even rattled. But then it was as if someone threw a switch and the competitor in them rose to the occasion. Just like that, they'd find a way to channel their anger and make it work for them.

Kyle was doing that now. He went to work on Sammy, still throwing hard, but not crazy-fast, as he had been doing. Sammy hung in there and worked the count to 3-and-2 before fouling off three pitches in a row. Then Kyle blew a fastball past him for strike three.

The Orioles groaned.

One out.

"THAT'S OKAY, SAMMY! KEEP YOUR HEAD UP!" a voice from the stands cried. Corey realized it was his dad. He peeked out from the corner of the dugout and saw his dad drape an arm around Mr. Noah. Mr. Noah didn't look too upset about Sammy striking out, but Joe Maduro seemed to be saying something encouraging to him anyway.

Corey smiled and shook his head. Who is this guy? he wondered as he grabbed his bat and headed to the on-deck circle.

Mickey was up next. But Kyle seemed locked in now, and the Orioles catcher flailed at two chest-high fastballs. With the count 2-and-1, the Norfolk pitcher finished him off with a big, sweeping curve that just caught the outside corner for strike three.

Two outs.

As Mickey trudged disconsolately back to the dugout,

Corey took a deep breath and tossed aside the weighted bat.

It all felt like a dream now, the kind of dream he'd had ever since he was a little kid: game on the line, Corey Maduro coming to the plate, the Orioles on the top step of their dugout, screaming themselves hoarse, the fans of both teams on their feet and cheering madly.

Yet the Orioles could see that Kyle had his confidence back, too. He strutted around the mound, grinning at his teammates and slamming the ball over and over into his glove. Then he turned to Katelyn at second base and waved.

She didn't wave back.

She didn't smile this time, either.

Instead, she stuck her tongue out at him. Now everyone in the ballpark seemed to be laughing as Kyle's face reddened and his grin disappeared.

Thanks, Katelyn, Corey thought ruefully. Tick him off even more. Just what I need.

Digging in, Corey heard his dad's voice again, rising above the din: "HERE WE GO, SON! NICE LEVEL SWING! YOU CAN DO IT!"

This voice was different from the one he'd heard from his dad all these months. It wasn't harsh. It wasn't sarcastic. It didn't sound desperate, the way it had so many other times this season, as if his dad would die right then and there if Corey didn't get a hit and the Orioles didn't win.

This voice was the best one he'd heard since his mom died.

Corey had the urge to step out and look up at his dad

and do one of those corny things major leaguers do, like tap his heart twice to say, "Luv you, man!"

But there was no time for that. Kyle was staring in at his catcher, waiting for the sign. And thanks to Katelyn sticking out her tongue, he looked like he wanted to throw the ball *through* Corey, not past him.

The first fastball came right at Corey's chin and sent him sprawling in the dirt.

He got up quickly and eyed the stands, hoping his dad wouldn't go crazy and yell something horrible at the pitcher or the Red Sox coach—or do something even worse. But Joe Maduro was still in his seat, looking concerned, but nothing more.

Good, Corey thought. He dusted himself off and peered at Kyle, who stared balefully back at him. That pitch, Corey knew, had been solely to intimidate him. Now the kid would be trying to get him out. The next pitches would all be around the plate.

Kyle looked in for the sign and checked Katelyn at second base. In that instant, Corey made up his mind: *If it's anywhere close, I'm swinging.*

Now the pitch was on its way. Corey tried to start his swing early, but this was maybe the fastest pitch he had ever seen in his life. Forget seventy miles per hour. This one was more like eighty. It felt more like major-league heat.

He was late getting the bat around, real late. But somehow he got a piece of it, the ball pinging off the end of the bat as he hit a little flare—a "dying quail," his dad always called these—over the first baseman's head.

Kyle knew it was trouble right away. He had a look of horror on his face as the ball hung in the air for what seemed like forever before dropping in front of the charging right fielder.

Corey was already halfway down the line, running harder than he ever had. He crossed the bag and turned in time to see Katelyn steaming across the plate, hands held high in celebration.

Game over.

Orioles 1, Red Sox 0.

Katelyn whipped off her helmet and ran toward him with her arms open, screaming, "Corey, you did it!" And the rest of the Orioles were streaming out of the dugout, whooping and cheering and bearing down on him, too.

In the instant before they got to him, Corey thought: Here goes nothing. He looked up in the stands, where the Orioles fans were hugging and high-fiving one another, and caught his dad's eye.

Then he tapped his heart. Twice.

He saw his dad's eyes widen and a big smile creased his rugged, tanned face.

Corey looked up at the heavens and tapped his heart again. "For you, Mom," he whispered.

Then he disappeared in a jubilant, swirling mob of Orioles.

Sammy and Gabe found Corey at a table in the back of the hotel ballroom, looking at the plaque he had just received for making the all-tournament team. They wasted no time teasing him unmercifully.

"Shine that up for you, Mr. Maduro, sir?" Sammy said, grabbing a napkin and pretending to buff the plaque.

"And will you be signing autographs later, Mr. Maduro?" Gabe said. "All your fans want to know. Lines will be long, but don't worry, we'll have extra security on hand. In fact, they're setting up the velvet ropes right now."

"Four hits, three doubles, four RBIs—you were brilliant, sir!" Sammy gushed. "Absolutely brilliant!"

"And don't forget the catch against the Indians!" Gabe said. "It's already immortalized on *SportsCenter* as one of the greatest defensive plays of all time."

Corey grinned sheepishly. "Apparently whoever voted on these awards forgot about that little adventure I had in the ivy," he said. "The one that cost us the game against the Blue Jays."

"Oh, that wasn't really your fault, Corey," a voice said.

They turned to see Katelyn plop down at the table, carrying her own all-tournament plaque. Corey's grin got wider.

He was happy for Katelyn. No one deserved a plaque more than she did for the "called-shot" grand slam that beat the Indians. Not to mention that strategic little mind game she played with Kyle VanderMeer that led to the walk, and the steal that led to the winning run against the Red Sox.

"No," she continued, "that ivy was so thick it should have been illegal. If the ivy's like that in the real Wrigley Field, they should burn it all down. And how could anyone know there was a board with a nail back there? You were lucky you didn't slice your hand open trying to get that ball."

She sighed and a dreamy look came over her. "You were so brave trying to make that play!" she said. "And there I was, saying all those nasty things to you. I was just the most awful person! Can you ever forgive me?"

As Corey's cheeks turned crimson, Sammy and Gabe looked at each other and rolled their eyes.

"Oh . . . my . . . God!" Sammy murmured. "This is *so* making me ill."

Just then, to Corey's great relief, his dad appeared at his side.

"Take a walk with your old man?" Joe Maduro asked, smiling. Then to the others: "Can I steal this superstar away from you for a few minutes?"

Corey nodded and practically bolted from the chair. "Here, hold on to this," he said, handing Sammy the plaque and muttering, "Uh, Katelyn, I gotta go. Congrats on your award."

Corey and his dad left the ballroom and strolled outside to the back patio. It was almost ten o'clock, and the moon was a big orange ball hanging low in the sky.

The weather forecast for the next day called for temperatures near a hundred degrees with sticky conditions. But right now a cool ocean breeze was beating back the humidity and making it one of the most pleasant nights of their stay.

"We haven't had a chance to talk," his dad began. "Wow, buddy, you made all-tournament! I'm so proud of you."

"Thanks, Dad," Corey said. "But I got a little lucky, too."

"No, you didn't," his dad said. "You had a great week down here."

He paused and swallowed hard. "I just want you to know I'm sorry. For everything."

Corey nodded and squeezed his dad's shoulder.

"That video," his dad continued, shaking his head. "It just *shocked* me. To see me doing that stuff during your game . . . I was so embarrassed I couldn't even talk about it. Couldn't even look at you without feeling this tremendous guilt for letting you down."

Corey said nothing. He stared out into the darkness, sensing his dad had more to say.

"I don't know when I started taking your games so seriously," Joe Maduro went on. "Maybe it was right around the time your mom got sick. I was so worried about her. Your games took my mind off her for a couple of hours. I guess that's why they became so important to me."

Yeah, the same thing happened to me, Corey admitted silently.

"I just wanted you to do well. And I got too wrapped up in it, became way too hard on you and the team and . . ." His voice trailed off. He shook his head, as if trying to clear away the bad memories. "Anyway," he declared, "that's over with."

When he saw Corey's skeptical expression, he added hastily, "Okay, I'll *try*, at least. I wish I could guarantee that I'll never act like a jerk again, but—"

"I know," Corey interrupted gently. "There are no guarantees in life. You told me that when Mom died, remember?"

His dad nodded. "That's right, I did say that."

"You also said you were glad we had her for as long as we did, even though it was painful in the end," Corey continued.

His dad kept nodding, but slowly now, as if unsure about where Corey was heading.

"Well," Corey said, "even though this week was painful sometimes—and I mean *really* painful—I'm still glad you were here."

His dad smiled gratefully, and Corey saw a tear roll down his cheek. "Thank you, buddy. Will you . . . will you give me one more chance? One more chance to be a better dad?"

How many times had Corey heard these words? A half dozen? More? But something in his dad's face told him the man was serious this time. Something told him that after all these months, Joe Maduro finally got it.

"Sure, Dad," he said, giving him a big hug. When they parted, his father looked like he might faint or cry or maybe do both.

Instead, Joe Maduro took a deep breath and said, "Okay, now I have to go back inside. Still have some unfinished business to take care of."

"Unfinished business?" Corey said.

"Yeah," his dad said. "I need to apologize to Coach for how I acted. And to the other parents. I spoke to some of them at the game. Spoke to a few of the others here right before the awards ceremony, too."

Corey's eyes widened. His dad was a proud man, not the type to readily admit he was wrong, especially to other adults he didn't know well.

"How did that go?" Corey asked.

His dad shrugged. "Some of them were great about it," he said. "Better than I deserved. Way better. Others didn't want to hear it. They're still royally pissed at me and they made that clear. Can't say I blame them."

He looked down at Corey with a sad smile. "But maybe someday they'll see that I've changed. Maybe someday I can convince them I'm not a world-class jerk anymore."

"Dad?" Corey said, looking up. "You convinced me."

His dad hugged him again.

"Then I'm off to a great start," he said. "C'mon, let's go inside."

30

They were sixty miles north of Sea Isle, traveling along the coastal highway back to Baltimore, when the driver of the eighteen-wheeler in the merge lane flicked on his left-turn signal.

"Better let this truck in, Joe," Mr. Noah said casually.

"What truck?" Joe Maduro said.

He peered through the windshield and swiveled his head back and forth, as if searching for another vehicle. Next he took off his glasses and examined them, before shrugging and putting them back on.

"There's a truck out there?" he said. "I don't see anything."

Corey, Sammy, and Mr. Noah looked on with alarm.

"Dad!" Corey shouted. "You're telling us you don't see that—"

Suddenly Corey's dad burst out laughing and shouted, "Got you! Oh, I got you all good that time!"

He quickly moved over to allow the truck to merge safely, and the driver thanked him with a crisp wave.

"Okay, you sure did," said Mr. Noah, the color returning to his face. "We thought you'd gone blind for sure."

Corey couldn't remember the last time he'd seen his dad in such a good mood. Not only that, but in the hour or so that they'd been on the road, his dad had yet to bring up baseball and the tournament.

Instead, the four of them had talked about everything else they'd experienced in their week in North Carolina, from the sun and the ocean and the barbecue to Gusher World and even Freddy the Gator.

"Speaking of Freddy," Sammy said, "I never believed there was a twelve-foot man-eating alligator in that pond."

Corey snorted. "Seriously? Dude, you were terrified! You looked like you thought Freddy was going to leap the fence and tear your head off! Like he was Supergator or something."

"Okay, I was a *little* worried that he might *possibly* exist," Sammy said. "But with my lightning speed and cat-quick reflexes, he wasn't going to get me. Besides, my plan was to throw Justin at Freddy as a diversion."

"You mean as a snack." Joe Maduro chuckled. "I'm sure Justin would have appreciated that."

Finally it was Mr. Noah who turned to the two boys in the backseat and asked, "So how do you think the team did in Sea Isle?"

Before they could answer, Corey's dad said, "A three–two record in a field with some of the top teams in the East? Against some terrific pitching? That's nothing to be ashamed of. You guys did great."

Corey nodded. "For our first big tournament away from home, I thought we did pretty well. We were in every game, even the two we lost."

"Absolutely," Sammy said. "And the last game was the best. The VanderMeer twins—those guys were nasty! Fastest pitchers we ever faced by far. And we didn't back down."

"We hung in there and found a way to win," Corey agreed. "That's huge. That'll give us a lot of confidence for the rest of the season."

"And let's not forget the biggest thing that happened in Sea Isle," Sammy said.

They all looked at him quizzically.

"Trumpets, please!" said Sammy. "The best thing that happened was—ta-da!—Corey found a girlfriend!"

As Sammy hooted and the two men in the front seat cracked up, Corey could feel his face getting hot.

"Let me make a car-wide announcement right now," he said. "She is *not* my girlfriend. Not even close."

But Sammy wasn't letting go of this one. "Here's where I see this relationship going," he began.

"There *is* no relationship," Corey said. "I thought we cleared that up."

"What'll probably happen first," Sammy continued, "is a couple of casual dates. Then—*boom!*—you'll take her to the prom."

"Really? The prom?" Corey said. "How many twelve-year-olds go to a prom, Sammy? Is that a pretty extensive list?"

Sammy pretended not to hear him. "It'll be pretty expensive, too," he said. "Tickets, tuxedo rental, corsage for her, photos—it all adds up. At least that's what I hear. But, hey, don't think about the money, bro. I'm sure the two of you will have a great time."

"Read my lips: You're crazy," Corey said.

"Then I suppose the next step will be marriage," Sammy said.

"Right from the prom to marriage?" Mr. Noah said with a grin. "Can't they date for a few more years? Get to know each other a little?"

"And what about college?" Corey's dad said. "Can't they go there before getting married?"

"Guys, please!" Sammy said. "You're messing up my narrative here!"

"Sorry," Mr. Noah said. "Okay, so they go right from being outfielders on the same team to the prom to marriage?"

"Correct," Sammy said. "Then after a few years, of course, it's time to have k—"

"Shut it!" Corey said, grinning. "Shut it right now!"

"See?" Sammy cackled. "Now he's even starting to *talk* like Katelyn! Pretty soon he'll be calling everyone *nerd* and punching people in the shoulder."

"And I'll start with you, nerd!" Corey said, firing a jab that Sammy blocked.

All four of them laughed so hard that the two men in the front seat had to wipe tears from their eyes.

"Keep your eyes on the road, Dad," Corey said when he finally caught his breath.

Joe Maduro squinted out the windshield. "Road?" his dad said. "What road? Is there a road out there?"

They all cracked up again. Corey looked at his dad's happy face in the rearview mirror and thought:

Best road trip ever.

If you enjoyed this book, look for

OUT AT HOME

a novel by
CAL RIPKEN, JR.
with Kevin Cowherd

Coming in Winter 2015